mary-kateandashley

Sweet 16

D0996143

Look for these
Sweet 16
titles:

1 Never Been Kissed
2 Wishes and Dreams
3 The Perfect Summer
4 Getting There
5 Starring You and Me

mary-kateandashley

Sweet 16

MY BEST FRIEND'S BOYFRIEND

Rosalind Noonan

■ HarperCollins*Entertainment*
An Imprint of HarperCollins*Publishers*

A PARACHUTE PRESS BOOK

A PARACHUTE PRESS BOOK
Parachute Publishing, LLC
156 Fifth Avenue
Suite 325
NEW YORK
NY 10010

First published in the USA by HarperEntertainment 2002
First published in Great Britain by HarperCollins*Entertainment* 2005
HarperCollins*Entertainment* is an imprint of HarperCollins*Publishers* Ltd,
77-85 Fulham Palace Road, Hammersmith, London W6 8JB

SWEET 16 books are created and produced by Parachute Press, LLC, in
cooperation with Dualstar Publications, a division of Dualstar Entertainment Group,
LLC, published by HarperEntertainment, an imprint of HarperCollins Publishers.

The HarperCollins website address is
www.**fire**and**water**.com

1 3 5 7 9 8 6 4 2

The author asserts the moral right to be
identified as the author of the work.

ISBN 0 00 718098 5

Printed and bound in Great Britain by Clays Ltd, St Ives plc

chapter one

"Lauren is definitely hiding something," I told my sister, Ashley, as we dropped our trays on our regular table in the cafeteria. It was a rainy Monday afternoon, and the room was crowded and noisy.

Ashley shook her head. "I don't get it," she said. "How can you be so sure?" She opened up her bottle of water and took a sip.

Our friend, Brittany Bowen, sat down across from us and shrugged off her red cardigan. "Mary-Kate is right," she said. "Hold on to your headbands, girls, and listen to this." Her chunky earrings swung wildly as she looked around for any sign of Lauren. Then she leaned forward and said in a low voice, "Yesterday, I caught Lauren in a lie!"

"No way!" I said. I took a bite of my mac and cheese. "What about?"

"Are you sure, Britt?" Ashley looked doubtful. "You know Lauren doesn't like to lie."

"That's true," I said. Lauren is one of the sweetest girls we know, with an always positive outlook. Besides, her pale, freckled skin turned fire-engine red whenever she tried to tell even the tiniest of white lies.

Brittany nodded. "Yeah, I know. She's really bad at it. But I called Lauren's house yesterday afternoon, and her mom said she was at the mall—with *Tashema!*" She widened her big brown eyes and looked from Ashley to me expectantly.

I scrunched up my face. "And that would be a problem because . . . ?"

"Because Tashema has piano lessons on Sunday afternoons," Brittany explained. "There was no way she could be at the mall with Lauren."

Ashley took a bite of her salad and chewed thoughtfully. "So let's say Lauren *is* hiding something from us. What do you think it is?"

"A secret life?" I joked. "Maybe she just found out she's a princess, like in that book."

Brittany laughed. "Yeah, and she's the new heir to the throne of Genovia. That would explain her new haircut—it's part of her royal makeover!"

"Hmmm . . ."

I looked up. Ashley had that faraway look in her eyes that meant she was trying to figure something out. Her face lit up. "Oh, my gosh! Maybe it's a boy."

"No way," I said. "Why would she keep that a secret from us?"

"Yeah," Brittany said. "We're her best friends. Whenever Lauren likes a guy, I'm the first to know about it."

"But she's never had a serious boyfriend," Ashley said. "You know how shy she is with guys. Maybe she met someone she really likes. And she wants to keep it to herself for a while."

"Well, I don't know about you, but the suspense is killing me," Brittany said. "We have to find out what's going on before I explode!"

A sneaky thought crept into my head. "Hey! Why don't we follow her after school today?"

Brittany put down her fork and stared at me. "That's a great idea—we'll be spy girls!"

"Cool!" I gave her a high five.

Ashley shook her head. "I hate to bring this up, but don't you two have rehearsal today?"

I sighed. "Don't remind me. We have less than two weeks left until opening night!"

We were putting on a production of *Grease* and I was playing the part of Sandy, the female lead. As vice president of the drama club, I wanted it to be the best show Bayside High School has ever seen.

Brittany glanced over my shoulder. "Here comes Lauren."

A few seconds later, Lauren rushed up to our table. "Hey, guys! Sorry I'm late," she said. "Mr. Skidmore asked me to drop off some things at the office for him." She slid into the seat next to Brittany and pulled a tuna sandwich and some carrot sticks from her lunch bag.

"Hi, Lauren!" we all chimed.

"So, what were you guys talking about?" Lauren asked.

"The play," I answered. "I'm getting a little nervous about opening night."

"What could you possibly have to be nervous about?" Lauren asked. "You're going to be a great Sandy. Nathan is the perfect Danny. And you even managed to get Danielle Bloom to play Rizzo! She's so talented."

"And the fact that her mother is Diana Donovan doesn't hurt, either," Brittany said. "The daughter of an Oscar-winning actress is going to be in our play? Who can beat that?"

I nodded. "I know, I know!" I said. "And even though she's still got an attitude—always going around saying that she studied acting with 'very famous coaches'—she's been terrific in rehearsals."

"How's Jake doing with his part?" Ashley asked.

"Great!" I smiled as I thought about my boyfriend, Jake Impenna, a senior here at Bayside. He was gorgeous, athletic, and totally sweet. Even though he wasn't into acting, he was playing a small part in the show—just so we could spend time together.

"Oh, Mary-Kate, I might not be able to make it to the stage crew meeting after school today," Lauren said. "Could you tell Damon when you see him?"

Ah-ha! Here was Lauren mysteriously backing out of yet another activity. Brittany raised one of her perfectly shaped eyebrows and gave me a meaningful look.

"Sure, Lauren," I said. "I don't think Damon's ordered the supplies for the sets yet, so it should be okay." Damon Williams was in charge of the stage crew.

Brittany snatched one of Lauren's carrot sticks. "So, Lauren," she said casually, "if you're not going to the meeting, what *are* you going to be doing after school today?"

Lauren stared down at her sandwich. "Ummm . . . nothing much," she said. "I have to get home."

"Really?" I leaned forward. "Why?"

"I—uh—I have to help my little sister," Lauren stammered. "Kermit, her pet gerbil, is loose in the house again, and I need to find him."

It was such a lame story that even Ashley was looking at Lauren suspiciously.

"Poor Kermit!" Brittany said. "He must be so scared! Do you want us to come over and help you look for him?"

"No!" Lauren yelped. "I mean—I've got it covered. But thanks, anyway."

I gave Brittany a wink. That settled it. Operation Super Spy was in effect. We'd just do it *after* rehearsal. We were going to find out what Lauren was hiding—no matter what!

chapter two

For the rest of lunch period, Mary-Kate and Brittany tried to get Lauren to spill her secret. Poor Lauren! She was going to have the two of them shadowing her everywhere.

I had to admit that I was curious, too. *Was* Lauren hiding something? And why? Then I thought, maybe she just needed some time to herself. There wasn't anything wrong with that. I finished my salad and stood up.

"Hey, Ashley, can you toss this for me, please?" Lauren asked. She handed me her empty soda can.

"No problem," I said. "I'll do cleanup today. Here, everyone, pile your stuff on this tray." Mary-Kate and Brittany gave me their lunch wrappers, and I started toward the recycling bins. As I walked by the rowdy group of guys at the next table, I glanced over to see who was making all the noise.

Sam McHugh and his friends. I should have known. They were always fooling around. It was too bad—with his curly black hair and brown eyes, Sam was kind of cute. But he never took anything seriously. *Not* good boyfriend material.

I dumped my tray and headed back to our table, dodging the balled-up paper napkins flying through the air. Suddenly, Sam zoomed past me, almost knocking me over.

"Hey!" I squeaked in surprise.

Sam glanced back at me over his shoulder and yelled, "Sorry, Ashley!"

Evan Rundo streaked by a second later, running after Sam.

"Better get out of the way, Ashley," Brittany called to me. "Those two were suspended last month for wrestling in the halls."

"You're toast, McHugh!" Evan yelled at the top of his lungs.

I hurried back to our table and sat down. Mary-Kate shook her head. "Those guys are bad news—big time."

"Hey, Rundo!" Sam yelled. "How about some salad?" He scooped a spoonful of salad from someone's bowl and flicked it at Evan.

It hit Evan right in the face. Everyone laughed as Russian dressing dripped down his cheek. Kids cheered, urging Sam and Evan on. Evan grabbed a slice of pizza from the table in front of him. "Take that, idiot!" He hurled the pizza at Sam.

Sam turned—too late! The pizza slice hit Sam in the middle of his back.

"Oh! You got me!" Sam croaked. He fell to his knees dramatically. Then, he snatched a burger from the hands of the boy sitting next to him. "Eat this!" He threw the burger at Evan.

We watched as it sailed through the air. Evan ducked, just in the nick of time. The greasy, ketchup-laden patty flew behind him—

And hit Ms. Greenberg, the assistant principal!

"Oooh!" I winced. "That is *really* bad news."

But Sam was totally cool. "Oh, hi, Ms. Greenberg," he said casually. "You want fries with that burger?"

The cafeteria exploded with laughter. Even I had to stifle a giggle.

Ms. Greenberg walked over to Sam. She clapped one hand on his shoulder, one hand on Evan's, and steered them both out of the cafeteria.

Mary-Kate frowned. "Sam acts like he *wants* to get in trouble."

"Well, looks like he got what he wanted," Brittany said, gathering up her things.

Brrrriiiing! Over our heads, the first bell rang.

"See you at rehearsal, Britt," Mary-Kate called. She grabbed her backpack and headed for the exit. "Catch you guys later."

"Right. And good luck finding Kermit, Lauren," Brittany teased. "Call me if you need help."

Lauren ignored the dig. She just smiled and waved as we headed off to our lockers. Mine is the farthest from the lunchroom, and I jogged down the hall to beat the second bell. I needed to dump the books from my morning classes and load up on my trigonometry notebook, my history textbook, and my English lit—

"Oof!" I smacked right into a guy who stopped short in front of me. "Sorry," I said, hitching my backpack up on my shoulder. "I didn't see you."

The guy in front of me turned. I gasped. I couldn't believe it!

It was my ex-boyfriend, Ben Jones!

chapter three

"Ben?" I blinked. Was I seeing things? What would Ben be doing in my school? He went to Harrison High across town. But there was no mistaking Ben's dark brown eyes, his wide smile, and the way he tilted his head to one side when he was listening to you.

"Ashley! Hey, how's it going? Thrown any wild parties lately?" he joked.

"Oh, sure," I answered, still in shock. "Every night." Ben was my date for my sweet sixteen party. He was sporting a new haircut and was even cuter than I remembered. "What are you doing here?"

"Going to class," he said. "I just transferred to Bayside."

"No way! Really?" I asked.

"Yup." He nodded. "My folks decided to move, so here I am. Actually, I think I'm late for gym."

"I can show you where the gym is," I said. "I've got trig over in that direction. And you've got a good excuse to be late. First day and all."

"Lead the way," Ben said as we headed down the corridor. "It's weird being the new guy in the middle of the year. I mean, in September a lot of people are feeling their way around. But now I'm the only one who's lost."

"You'll get the hang of it," I said. I was so happy to see him! I really liked Ben. Things didn't work out for us as a couple, but we'd ended it well. And now that he was here, we'd be seeing each other around. It would be nice to have a chance to be friends. "If you want, I'll show you around sometime," I offered.

"That would be great," Ben said as we passed the bulletin board outside the gymnasium.

The second bell was ringing as I pointed to the side of the gym. "That's the entrance to the boys' locker room."

"Thanks, Ashley," Ben said, heading toward the door. "We'll catch up later. I'll see you in the cafeteria or something."

"Sure!" I waved, then hurried over to my locker. As I spun the lock, I thought about Ben. He always made me laugh. How great to have a chance to hang out with him!

Monday afternoon I sat in the auditorium, studying my lines. A voice broke into my thoughts. "T minus two weeks until opening night, Mary-Kate. How're you doing with your lines?" I glanced up as my boyfriend, Jake, slid into the seat next to me.

"I'm great," I told him. "Even better now that you're here." He slipped his arm around my shoulders and gave me a quick peck on the cheek.

"How about you?" I asked, squeezing Jake's hand. "Are you nervous about being in your first play?"

Jake shrugged. "I think I can handle being onstage for, like, ten minutes. Especially since I don't have any lines."

"Hello, everyone! I'm here!" a girl's voice announced. I didn't have to turn to know that Danielle Bloom had entered the auditorium.

"Hey, Danielle," I said as the petite red-haired girl flopped into the seat in front of mine.

"I have all my lines memorized," she said. "How about you, Mary-Kate?"

"I'm getting there." I smiled. "I'll definitely have it all down pretty soon." *I'd better*, I thought.

"How do you memorize all this dialogue?" Jake said, flipping through my script. I had highlighted all my lines with pink marker—and some of the pages were totally covered in pink!

"I just take it one scene at a time," I said.

"I'm into method acting," Danielle said. "My acting coach says you really have to throw yourself into the part. Feel the emotion. Experience Rizzo's pain."

Jake winked at me. "I haven't read the entire script yet, but how much pain does Rizzo's character feel?" he asked. "Does she get hit by a motorcycle or something?"

I choked back a laugh.

"Ha-ha," Danielle said. She shot Jake a look, then turned around in her seat.

Jake gestured toward my script. "Do you want some help memorizing your last few scenes?" he asked me. "We could meet up one night this week and work on it together."

I smiled. "That would be great. How about tomorrow, after basketball practice? That way we can—"

"Did I miss anything?" Brittany asked breathlessly. She dropped into the chair next to Jake's and fanned her face with her script. "Sorry I'm late. I saw you-know-who on the way over here and couldn't resist following her."

Jake looked interested. "Who's 'you-know-who?'"

"It's Lauren," I explained. "We think she's keeping a secret from us, and we want to find out what it is."

"Why don't you just ask her about it?" Jake said.

Brittany rolled her eyes. "Boys. They just don't understand, do they?"

I chuckled. "So what did you find out?"

"*Nada*," Brittany admitted. "It looked like Melanie was giving her a ride home. I'll call to check on her later."

I nodded. "Good idea."

The doors of the auditorium swung open and Mr. Owen, our drama club adviser, entered the room.

"Okay, people," Mr. Owen called out. "Take a seat and let's get down to business." He climbed onstage and waited for everyone to settle down. "We've got a few developments to discuss before we start rehearsal."

Developments? I leaned forward. What kind of developments was Mr. Owen talking about?

"First, some bad news," he said. "I'm afraid we've lost our set designer and chief carpenter, Damon Williams."

What? I thought as I looked around the auditorium for Damon. *Oh, no!*

A knot formed in the pit of my stomach. As vice president of the drama club, overseeing the sets was part of *my* job. *I* was the one who asked Damon to get involved in the stage crew—because he was one of the best artists in school. What could have gone wrong?

"Principal Needham just informed me that Damon injured his back during tennis practice today. He may be out of school for some time, so he won't be able to build our sets for *Grease*," Mr. Owen explained.

The auditorium was silent as everyone soaked in the information. I bit my lip. I turned to find the drama club president, Nathan Sparks, sitting a few rows behind me. I gave Nathan a desperate look that said, "What now?" He shrugged back.

"We were relying on Damon," Mr. Owen went on. "And now we need a volunteer to take over. So—is anyone able to help out?"

No one said a word. I glanced around, desperate. Seconds ticked by. Why was no one volunteering? *I worked hard to get the lead in this play*, I thought. *And I can't let anything stand in the way now!* I took a deep breath and stood up. "I'll do it, Mr. Owen!"

"Are you sure you have time, Mary-Kate?" Mr. Owen asked. "You may be taking on too much."

"We have a great stage crew," I said. "I know that we can pull together to get the sets built for opening night."

Mr. Owen smiled. "Thank you for your dedication, Mary-Kate. It seems the drama club can always depend on you."

I smiled back and sat down. That's when it hit me.

I couldn't believe I had just promised to help build the sets for the play. I wasn't exactly sure how I was going to do that, but this play was too important. I had to try.

Christy Turrel raised her hand. Her silver bracelets jangled down her arm. Two weeks ago, I had asked Christy to design and sew all of our costumes.

"Mr. Owen?" Christy said, peering through her long blond bangs, "I just want to report that I'll have two samples for everyone to look at in a few days. And I am completely on schedule to have everyone's outfits ready for opening night."

I sighed with relief. At least one part of the production was going smoothly. Christy had a real flair for fashion. I couldn't wait to see what she came up with.

"Thank you, Christy," Mr. Owen said. Then he took a deep breath. "All right, I've got one more announcement. Christopher, who was supposed to play Eugene, has dropped out of the show. I've brought in a replacement. I hope you'll all give a big Rydell High welcome to our new Eugene . . . Sam McHugh!"

I blinked. Sam McHugh? That clown? Was Mr. Owen kidding?

Sam shuffled his way from the back of the auditorium to the front of the stage. He lifted his fingers in a peace sign, and a few kids laughed. As everyone clapped to welcome Sam, Jake whispered in my ear, "Good luck getting McHugh to follow the script. He's a total joker."

Sam hopped up on the stage and Mr. Owen tossed him a script.

Sam juggled the book dramatically—and it fell to the floor. "Oops!"

"That's okay. I'll get it." Mr. Owen bent to pick up the script. Once again he handed it to Sam.

"Whoa! Whoooa!" Sam dropped the book again. It hit the stage floor in a crumpled pile. "Sorry," he said. He held up his hands and gave everyone in the audience a big smile. "I've got butterfingers!"

Half the cast burst into laughter, but I was fuming. Why did he always have to act like such a jerk?

Mr. Owen frowned. "Okay, people! Let's rehearse our opening number. We want the T-Birds and the Pink Ladies onstage. That includes Danny and Eugene, and the kids of Rydell High."

There was a flurry as everyone took their places. Jake found his mark on the left side of the stage with two other Rydell High "students."

Then the pianist started playing, and the cast began to sing.

Mr. Owen backed up the aisle. He kept his eyes on the stage as he watched the opening number. When he got to my seat, he paused.

"Mary-Kate, can I speak to you for a second?" he whispered.

"Of course," I answered. I followed him to the back of the auditorium.

"What's up, Mr. Owen?" I asked.

"I need a favor," he said in a low voice. "Since Sam is new to our production, I was wondering if you wouldn't mind giving him a little extra help."

"Me?" I already had my own lines to memorize, plus a gazillion sets to build. Not to mention a *life*, which included my friends and my boyfriend. When was I supposed to find time to help Sam?

I glanced up at the stage. Sam was swinging his arms wildly in time to the music—joking around, as usual. "I'm sorry, Mr. Owen," I said, "but I think you should find someone else to—"

"Mary-Kate," Mr. Owen interrupted. "I'm asking you because you're one of the most responsible people in the drama club. You can set a good example for Sam. And I know that he can learn a lot from you."

"Thanks," I said. *I guess,* I added silently.

"Sam is in major trouble," Mr. Owen went on. "Just between us, detention hasn't made a difference in his behavior. Principal Needham thinks that a more positive approach will do the trick. I'm hoping that Sam won't see the show as a punishment—more like a second chance."

I squinted at the teacher. "So *this* is Sam's detention? Being in our show?"

Mr. Owen frowned. "It's a long, long story," he said. "Maybe you can get Sam to tell it to you sometime."

I doubted that. Sam wasn't exactly the sort of guy I'd want to trade secrets with.

Mr. Owen placed a hand on my shoulder. "That's why I was concerned earlier that you were taking on too much. If you want to reconsider heading up the stage crew, I'll understand."

"No, that's okay." I gulped. "I can handle it all. Really."

"Great!" Mr. Owen smiled. "I'll tell Sam about our arrangement. The sooner you two get started, the better for everyone."

"Right," I answered. My voice came out in a squeak. I glanced up at the stage again. Now Sam was doing a handstand.

I groaned. How did I get myself into this?

chapter four

"What was I thinking, Ashley?" Mary-Kate ripped another piece of paper from her notebook, crumpled it, and threw it to her bedroom floor. "How am I supposed to figure out how much wood and things we need to build these sets? I'm not a carpenter. I have no idea what I'm doing!"

"Maybe I can help." I sat down at the foot of her bed, trying to reassure her. I had never seen her so frazzled.

Mary-Kate crossed out another row of figures. "Aaarrrgh!" She held her forehead with her hand. "Save me, Ashley. I'm about to spontaneously combust!"

I took the notepad from her hand and placed it on the bed beside me. "Maybe if you calm down for a second, the answer will come to you," I suggested.

"Right. Calm. I'll try it." She took a couple of deep breaths.

After a minute or two she looked up at me. "Let's talk about something other than drama club. It might help to clear my mind."

"Okay." I smiled. I had been waiting for an opportunity to tell her about my afternoon. "Guess who I ran into at school today?"

Mary-Kate shrugged her shoulders. "I give up."

"Ben Jones," I told her.

Mary-Kate gasped. "No way! Ben Jones as in your ex-boyfriend?" she asked. "Where? How? What was he doing at Bayside High?"

"He moved here!" I said. "He was wandering the halls, looking for the gym, when I bumped into him—literally."

"I can't believe it. And last month you bumped into Brian at the mall," Mary-Kate said. "Is this some kind of cosmic coincidence or what?"

"I know," I admitted. "It's like I'm destined to keep running into boys I used to date. Next month I'll probably bump into Andrew Leonard—that kid I used to play with in kindergarten."

Mary-Kate giggled. "So what was it like to talk to Ben again?"

"Great!" I said. "He's still a totally nice guy. I told him I'd give him the grand tour of Bayside High."

"You know, you always had fun with Ben," Mary-Kate pointed out. "It'll be nice having him around."

I nodded. Ben was definitely fun. We just didn't have any chemistry together when we were going out. There weren't any sparks. So we decided we'd be better off as friends than boyfriend and girlfriend.

The phone rang, and Mary-Kate groaned. "You get it," she said, pulling her pillow over her head. "If it's Mr. Owen or anyone from drama club, tell them I ran away!"

I laughed and reached over to grab the receiver. "Hello?"

"I have a major news flash about Lauren," Brittany said.

"Hold on," I told her. "Let me put you on speakerphone." I pressed a button on the phone cradle and flopped down on Mary-Kate's bed.

"It's Brittany," I told my sister.

"Hey, Britt," Mary-Kate said. "What's up?"

"Are you sitting down?" Brittany's voice came through the speaker.

"Sure," I answered. "Where are you?"

"I'm at the mall," she said. "A few minutes ago, I called Lauren. And her mom told me that Lauren wasn't home—that she was baby-sitting tonight."

"And?" Mary-Kate prodded.

"And guess who just walked by?" Brittany said.

"Lauren!" Mary-Kate said. "So where is she now?"

"Headed for the CD store," Brittany reported. "I say we kick this operation into high gear. Get your butts down here, girls. We have some serious spying to do!"

I glanced at Mary-Kate. I still wasn't crazy about the idea of following Lauren around. But it would definitely take my sister's mind off her troubles. I grabbed the keys to our Mustang.

"Hang on, Brittany!" I said. "We are on our way!"

❀

Twenty minutes later, Ashley, Brittany, and I were hiding out at Curtains and Things in the mall. I peered through a set of dark wooden blinds at Lauren, who was sitting on a bench just outside the store, reading a magazine.

"Careful, Mary-Kate," Brittany warned. "We don't want Lauren to see us."

I flicked the blinds closed. "I don't think that's a problem," I reported. "She looks too involved in her magazine."

"So what's the deal?" Ashley asked. "Why would Lauren tell her mom she's baby-sitting when she's really coming to the mall to read?"

"Beats me." I shrugged.

"I smell a cover-up," Brittany said.

"And I smell doughnuts," I told her, stealing a glance at the food court. "And pretzels and popcorn and—"

"Hungry?" Ashley smiled. "I'll split a frozen yogurt with you."

"Excellent!" I said. "I'll go get it."

"But what if Lauren sees you?" Brittany asked.

"No problem," I answered. "Like all good spies, I came prepared." I flipped up the hood on my sweatshirt. Now my face and hair were hidden. I looked kind of ridiculous—but I was definitely unrecognizable.

"Be careful!" Ashley called.

I looked left and right, then carefully slipped out the door. I made it past Lauren without any problem. She never even glanced up. On the way to the yogurt stand, I flipped my hood down. That's when I noticed something out of the corner of my eye. Sam McHugh working at the Donut Hole, all decked out in a crisp white uniform and a paper hat.

As I passed, his eyes locked on me. *Guess I'd better say hello,* I thought. Sam and I were going to be spending a lot of time together, and I didn't want to start off on the wrong foot. Slowly, I approached the counter. "Hi, Sam. So, I hear we're—"

"Hey! Check it out, everyone!" Sam called to the other guys at the counter. "It's Mary-Kate Olsen—the Drama Queen of Bayside High!"

The boys behind the counter laughed at his joke.

"Yeah—um, hi," I said. "I just stopped by to tell you how happy we all are to have you in our show."

"Right," Sam said with a smirk. "Hey! I have an idea. Why don't you just call it a show-*off*? That's what you're all doing up there, anyway, right?"

The guys behind the counter snickered again.

Sam was making fun of me! I could feel my cheeks flushing red.

Sam continued, "Can you really call it a *show* if no one *shows* up to watch?"

That was it—why was I even wasting my time? The play was one of the most important things in my life right now. I wasn't going to stand here and listen to Sam McHugh trash it. I turned and walked toward the yogurt stand.

"Hey, Mary-Kate," Sam called after me. "Want me to *show* you out of the food court?"

I clenched my fists. What a jerk. I couldn't believe that I had to actually help that guy. *It's not for Sam,* I told myself. *It's for the good of the play. If you don't help him, Sam could ruin it—and you have worked too hard for that.*

I just hoped I'd be able to get through to him before opening night.

❀

"She's coming this way! Quick, Ashley! Put this on!" Brittany plopped a huge, wide-brimmed straw hat on top of my head. She grabbed a baseball cap for herself and jammed it down low on her brow. Just in time! A second later, Lauren strolled past the window of Hat's That.

Brittany peered out of the store entrance. "Oh, no!" She gasped. "She's headed for the food court! Get Mary-Kate on the phone—quick!"

I took out my cell phone and dialed Mary-Kate's number. She answered on the first ring. "Sorry, Ash. The line for yogurt is taking forever. What's up?"

"Lauren's headed in your direction!" I told her. "Find cover! Quick!"

"Okay. Meet me at the pretzel cart," Mary-Kate said. Then she hung up.

Brittany and I returned our hats and carefully made our way to the pretzel cart. Mary-Kate was already there. She was eating a pretzel.

"May I help you?" a girl in a blue-striped uniform asked as we approached the cart.

"No thanks," Brittany said. "We're just people-watching."

"So where is she?" I asked.

Brittany pointed Lauren out. She was sitting at a table by herself and flicking through a magazine.

"She's just sitting there," Mary-Kate said after a few minutes. "I hate to admit it, but maybe there's no big secret after all."

I shrugged. "It could be. I mean, maybe she wanted to spend some time alone. Maybe she needs more personal space. Or maybe—"

"You guys!" Brittany interrupted. "She's waving to someone."

"Where?" I asked. I ducked left and right, trying to peek around the girl working the pretzel cart.

"It's a guy!" Mary-Kate cried.

"He's walking up to the table," Brittany reported. "He's taking her hand . . ."

"They're *kissing!*" Mary-Kate exclaimed. "We were right! We were right! Lauren has a secret boyfriend!"

"Really?" I nudged Mary-Kate out of the way. I had to see this for myself.

Sure enough, there was Lauren, kissing a guy in the middle of the food court.

"Lauren has a boyfriend! Lauren has a boyfriend!" Brittany and Mary-Kate jumped up and down together, giddy with happiness.

Then the boy turned and sat down next to Lauren. All at once, I felt the air rush out of me. That was no ordinary guy Lauren was kissing.

It was Ben.

My ex-boyfriend.

chapter five

"Come on, Ashley, what's the big emergency?" Lauren asked me the next day on our way to the cafeteria.

I bit my lower lip, not wanting to spill the beans. "I've been sworn to silence," I told Lauren. "At least until we're all together."

"Now I'm *really* curious," Lauren said.

Not as curious as I am, I thought. My mind flashed back to the scene I had witnessed in the food court. Lauren kissing Ben. A million questions swam through my mind. Like—how long had this been going on? When did Lauren and Ben get together? And why didn't she tell me?

Lauren and I found Brittany and Mary-Kate at the entrance to the cafeteria. We bought our lunches and sat down at our usual table. I was about to take a sip of juice when Brittany blurted out, "We know everything!"

Lauren froze, holding a fork full of lasagna in midair. "What? What are you talking about?"

"We know *everything*, Lauren," Brittany repeated. "We knew you were up to something, and now we know what. Congratulations!"

Mary-Kate threw an arm over Lauren's shoulder and gave her a squeeze. "We're so happy for you and Ben!"

Lauren put her fork down. "Oh my gosh," she said. "How do you know?"

"We followed you at the mall yesterday." Brittany laughed. "We were watching you, and we saw everything. You! Ben! You *and* Ben."

"You guys!" Lauren pressed her hands to her red cheeks. "I can't believe this!"

"What do you expect when you try to hide something from your best friends?" Mary-Kate asked. "I mean, we had to find out eventually."

"I know," Lauren admitted. "It's just that . . . I wasn't sure how everyone would feel about my seeing Ben." Her big blue eyes were suddenly locked on mine.

I swallowed. So that's why Lauren kept her relationship with Ben a secret. She didn't want to hurt me. I reached across the table and squeezed her hand. "Lauren, I am completely happy for you. And I am *thrilled* you found someone you like enough to date."

"Thanks, Ashley. I can't tell you how relieved I am to hear you say that."

"Lauren's got a boyfriend!" Brittany chanted. "Tell us *everything*. How did you two get together?"

"It was in July—while Mary-Kate and Ashley were away at MusicFest and you were at your summer house," she explained to Brittany. "I was hanging out by myself on the beach, and Ben just walked by. We started talking, then we went for a Coke. And then we met again and . . ." She shrugged. "It just sort of happened."

"Well, I'm glad that mystery is solved," Brittany said.

Mary-Kate took a bite out of her apple. "And now that the word is out, we can all start hanging out again."

A huge smile lit Lauren's face. "That would be great! I've been going nuts trying to split my time between you guys and Ben."

"Why don't you invite Ben to the movies with us tomorrow night?" Mary-Kate suggested.

"Yes!" Brittany agreed. "It will be Mary-Kate and Jake, Ashley and me, and you and Ben."

"Okay, I'll ask him tonight," Lauren said, nodding.

I swallowed back the lump in my throat and wondered why I suddenly didn't feel like going. I wasn't into Ben anymore. And I was really happy for Lauren. So why was I so upset?

"Good work, Mary-Kate! You are a first-rate Sandy."

"Thanks, Mr. Owen." I smiled from ear to ear. We had just finished rehearsing the slumber party scene in *Grease*.

"Same for you, Danielle," Mr. Owen praised. "A flawless performance, as usual."

"No problem," Danielle said. "It's what I was born to do."

Beside me, Brittany groaned. "Does she ever give it a rest?" she whispered.

"No," I answered truthfully. "But you have to admit, she is an amazing actress."

"Let's start the next scene right away, please," Mr. Owen called out. "T-Birds, Danny, and Eugene onstage."

Brittany and I walked toward the wings as Nathan, Sam, and a couple of the other boys took their places. "Hey, Drama Queen," Sam called as I brushed past him. "What's up, your majesty?"

Ugh. I was *not* looking forward to our first practice session together this afternoon. Brittany and I sat down and watched as Nathan walked confidently onto the stage. Sam slouched a few feet away from him.

"Okay, let's move a little closer together, and let's get into character," Mr. Owen directed. He turned to Sam. "Eugene, you're supremely intelligent but a total nerd. Lacking in social graces. You'd rather eat worms than talk to girls. And you are the least cool person at Rydell High."

Sam turned away from the audience and pulled up his pants. When he turned back, the waist of his baggy jeans reached up to his armpits. Everyone burst out laughing.

"That's it!" Mr. Owen exclaimed. "All right, let's start with your scene, middle of page twelve."

The guys started to run their lines, reading from their scripts.

"'Dancin' just ain't my thing,'" Nathan said, playing the part of Danny Zuko.

Sam stared at his script, grinning. "No? Then how about a mosh pit?"

"Hold it!" Mr. Owen yelled. "Sam, the line is: 'But it's the Spring Fling! And there's a contest.' It's okay to improvise a bit, but we need to keep the scene focused."

The guys did the lines over. This time Sam used a whiny nerd voice for Eugene.

"'But it's the Spring Fling!'" he said. "'And there's a *coooooontest!*'" He said the last word with an annoying nasal drone. The entire cast laughed.

I was impressed. Sam could really hit the mark when he wanted to. But as they moved on, Sam botched his next line, and his next. I started losing patience. It was clear that Sam was screwing up his lines *on purpose*. He wasn't even trying to get them right.

"You have to admit, he's funny," Brittany whispered to me.

"Then Mr. Owen should give him his own stand-up act," I fumed. "He's ruining our show!"

Just then Mr. Owen turned to the audience and clapped his hands. "Okay, people," he said, "let's take a short break. Ten minutes. And then we'll tackle the end of Act One."

"Hold on a minute!" Christy Turrel called from the back of the auditorium. "I need to measure anyone who hasn't been fitted for costumes already!"

"Right!" Mr. Owen said. "If you aren't all set for a costume, see Christy."

Brittany and I headed over to see how Christy was doing. She was taking Danielle's measurements.

"I want a fat belt," Danielle stated. "But not too fat. I have photos from the original Broadway production. My mom has a friend who was in the chorus."

Christy didn't answer, but she was starting to look annoyed as Danielle kept listing her demands.

"The pink needs to be just right," Danielle said. "Some pinks make my skin look yellow. I need a red pink, you know what I mean?"

Christy stared at Danielle, her blue eyes icy. "I know what pink is. And if you don't mind, *I'm* the costume designer. I get to decide what pink to use, okay?" She bent down to measure Danielle's hemline.

Danielle put her hands on her hips. "Well, you don't have to get so snooty about it," she said. "I'm just trying to help you get it right."

Brittany and I grinned at each other. Typical Danielle!

"Ready to start?" I asked Sam later that afternoon. I really wanted to be watching Jake's basketball practice. Instead, I was stuck here with Sam.

Sam picked up his backpack. "No way. Mr. Owen has gone home. If we leave right now, he'll never know it. I'm out of here, Drama Queen."

"Hold it, Sam." I blocked his way as he started up the aisle. "I don't like this any better than you do. But I promised Mr. Owen that I'd help you, so we're going to practice. Got it?"

Sam groaned. "All right, all right, take it easy." He plunked into a chair in the aisle. "Where do you want to start?"

"How about Eugene's first lines," I suggested. "Page twelve."

Sam flipped through his script and found the page. I waited. But he just sat there, staring down.

"Well?" I was getting impatient.

"Well, what, Drama Queen?"

I took a deep breath and counted to ten. "Read the line, Sam!"

"Why don't you tell me how you want me to read it, your majesty? That way, I'll be sure to get it right."

I couldn't believe how sarcastic he was being! I snatched the script out of his hands. "Fine! I'll make this really easy for you," I told him. "I'll read the line exactly the way you should say it and you just repeat after me, okay?"

Sam shrugged. "Whatever."

I gritted my teeth. *Sam may not care about this play,* I told myself. *But you do. You have to go through with this.* I took a deep breath. "This scene is in the school lunchroom. Here's Eugene's first line."

Sam repeated the line. Relief flooded through me. At least he was starting to cooperate. I read the other players' lines, then gave Sam the next line for Eugene. Using that funny nasal voice from practice, Sam nailed it again. Soon we had finished the scene, and Sam had done a great job!

I blinked up at him. "That was perfect! You know, you could be really great at this if you weren't joking around all the time."

"Just read the lines, okay?" he snapped.

I glared at him. *What was his problem?*

"Mary-Kate!" I turned and saw Jake walking into the auditorium.

"Hi!" I greeted him.

"I thought you were going to meet me in the gym," Jake said, casting a glance at Sam. "Hey, McHugh."

"I was," I told him, "but Mr. Owen asked me to help Sam with his lines."

Sam nodded at Jake, then said, "I have to get going, anyway." He grabbed his backpack and jogged toward the door.

"Hey! Your script!" I called after him. I dangled the script between my fingers. "You'll never learn the rest of your lines without this."

"Right." Sam stepped toward me and snatched the book from my hands. "One more useless pile of paper to lug around."

"We'll meet again tomorrow," I told him. "There's no official rehearsal, but that doesn't mean we can't—"

"Okay, okay," Sam cut me off. "I'll meet you in the drama club office after class." He turned and disappeared out the door.

I looked after him and sighed. For a while there, Sam had seemed to be enjoying himself, really getting into the lines.

"What's his problem?" Jake asked.

"I wish I knew," I said, gathering my papers and sliding them into my backpack. "Right now I just want to get as far away from Sam McHugh as possible. So tell me, how did basketball practice go?"

"It was tough!" Jake kneeled beside me to help collect my papers. "Coach really gave us a workout. He thinks we're going to have the best season ever."

"That's great!" I exclaimed. Then a wave of worry washed over me. I wished I could say the same for our show. So far, I hadn't gotten anywhere with the sets, and I'd made only the tiniest bit of progress with Sam. Could I possibly pull everything together by opening night?

chapter six

"Oh, Ashley, I'm so glad you're okay about Ben and me," Lauren said. "I was worried sick about how you'd react if you found out we were dating."

Lauren and I were at Starbucks, grabbing a Frappuccino after school on Wednesday. Lauren paid the cashier and grabbed her coffee. Then we sat at a table by the window.

"Of course I'm cool about it," I answered. "Ben's a great guy. I'm happy for you."

"It was so awful not being able to talk to you about him," Lauren admitted. "And I hated keeping him a secret."

"I can't believe you did it for so long," I said. "I mean, you even had Brittany fooled for a while."

Lauren winced. "I'm sorry. I should have trusted you guys. And I really should have been up-front with you, Ashley." She took a sip of her drink. "What was I thinking? You are such a good friend. I should have known that you'd understand."

I nodded. "It's no big deal, really. I really like Ben, but when we were dating, there just weren't any sparks between us."

"Yeah, that's what Ben said, too," Lauren told me.

I froze for a second. "Ben told you that?" I asked.

Lauren nodded as she sipped her coffee. "He said there was no chemistry. But that you're a really nice girl." She smiled.

I forced myself to smile back.

Lauren leaned forward, and her eyes lit up. "Ben's just so funny, and sweet. He brings me flowers and—oh, Ash, he's the most perfect boyfriend ever!"

"That's great, Lauren!" I said. "Your first real boyfriend. I'm so glad it's someone nice, like Ben."

"And now it's all out in the open," Lauren said. "Big sigh! Now we can do our Saturday afternoon study dates again. It's a lot more fun tackling poetry with you. Besides, this new Edgar Allan Poe poem has me cross-eyed!"

"'Quoth the raven, nevermore,'" I quoted.

Lauren laughed. "Everything's back to normal."

"You bet," I said, taking a sip of my Caffé Mocha. Everything was back to normal. So how come, inside, I felt anything *but* normal?

❋

Christy Turrel burst into the drama club office. "Mary-Kate! Have I got news for you!"

I looked up from my notebook. My latest attempt to figure out the materials we needed for the sets was not going well. "If it's good news, let me have it," I told Christy. "If it's bad news . . . don't bother."

"It's *great* news." Christy hopped up on my desk. The batik print of her flowy skirt billowed over my papers. "You are going to be so blown away when you see the costumes I've designed. I think I've even outdone myself this time!"

"That *is* good news! " I told her. "When do you think they'll be ready?"

"I'll have two sample costumes by the end of the week—one for Jan and one for Rizzo. That's Brittany and Danielle, right?"

"Right." I nodded.

Christy jiggled the beads on the end of her leather belt. "How about if we have the big unveiling at Saturday's rehearsal?" she suggested.

"Saturday is perfect!" I said, feeling a swell of excitement. "But will that give you enough time? We open next Thursday."

"No problemo!" Christy's sandals slapped the floor as she hopped down from my desk. "I'd better go. I've got some fringe to finish. Bye!"

"See you later!" I stared at the door for a moment after Christy left. Fringe? I wondered. Since when did people in the fifties wear fringe? *Oh well.* I shrugged. *Christy's the pro at clothing design. I have my own problems.*

I grabbed the Yellow Pages and flipped to the Hardware section. I ran my fingers down the columns until I found the entry I was looking for—Lindy's Home Store. It was where Mom bought all her picture frames.

I swallowed. Okay—I knew where to get the stuff for the sets. But now what? How much wood, canvas, and paint would I need? I glanced at the calendar tacked up on the office wall. Seven days . . . could that possibly be enough time?

"Knock, knock!" someone said, interrupting my thoughts. It was Sam McHugh. He threw his back- pack on the floor and groaned. "Torture time."

After Christy's enthusiasm, Sam's attitude was like a spray of cold water. I sighed. "I guess we should get started."

Sam came to the desk and glanced over my shoulder. "What're those?" he asked.

"I'm trying to figure out how much building material we'll need for the sets."

Sam picked up one of the sketches for the set design, then looked down at my calculations. "You're going to need twice that amount of wood," he told me. "You're only figuring length. You've got to add in height. Plus, you'll need even more lumber to brace the sets, and create stands for them. Otherwise, they just won't hold."

"Really?" I asked.

"Yeah, really," he answered. "And I wouldn't order from Lindy's. Too expensive. You'll end up going way over your budget. Get the wood, nails, and tacks from a lumberyard, and the paint and canvas from an art supply house. I can find a few numbers for you." He paged through the phone book to a different section and marked a few ads with Post-its.

Wow, Sam really seemed to have a handle on what he was doing. "How do you know all this stuff?" I asked.

"My dad's a carpenter," he said, flipping through my designs. "Sometimes I help him. And I like to mess around in his workshop. I build stuff in my spare time."

"What about nails?" I asked him.

"You want a cake of nails," he said. "And you need the materials fast, right?"

I nodded. He pointed to one of the entries in the phone book. "This place will deliver tomorrow if we order this afternoon. If you want, I'll talk to the hardware store for you. To make sure we get the right materials."

"That would be great, Sam," I said. "Thanks." I exhaled, feeling as if a tremendous weight had been lifted off my shoulders. I was actually making progress!

"Hey, Mary-Kate?" Jake came into the drama club office. His eyes were bright—until he took in the whole scene and noticed Sam. "Oh, hey there, McHugh. What's going on?"

Sam glanced up. "Not much, Impenna." He turned to me. "I'll go make this call, okay, Mary-Kate?"

"Thanks, Sam!" I said. Then I turned to Jake and gave him a kiss hello. "Hi! What are you doing here?"

"Sorry to interrupt," Jake said.

"It's okay," I told him. "We're ordering supplies for the sets. Sam's helping me." I looked at my watch. "Did they cancel your basketball practice?"

"No," Jake said, "I was just on my way over to the gym. I thought I'd see what you were up to."

"Just stuff for the play, as usual," I said, holding up one of the set designs. "Why don't we talk later?"

"Sure. Later," Jake agreed. He glanced at the back of Sam's head and rolled his eyes. Then he mouthed the words: "Good luck!"

After Jake left, I felt guilty. Sam wasn't turning out to be such a bad guy after all. "Thanks for doing this," I told him. "I really needed your help."

He nodded. "No problem." I think he was happy about being able to lend a hand, but with Sam it was hard to tell. He flopped into a chair and looked up at me with a goofy grin on his face. "Let's get this torture over with. Rehearse away."

I smiled back—for some reason, his joking didn't bother me that much today.

chapter seven

Little prickles of excitement formed on my arms as I watched Sam perform the scene we had rehearsed yesterday. Sam had really come through ordering the materials for our sets. And now he was even remembering his lines! Everything was falling into place.

"Psst! Mary-Kate!" Brittany whispered as she sat down next to me. "Looks like the supplies are here. Everything's ready to start building, I think."

"That's great!" I told Brittany. "Let's get the cast together after rehearsal. We're going to need everybody's help if we want to get these sets built in time."

"Good idea," Brittany said.

I watched as Sam finished his scene. Mr. Owen applauded and said, "Great job, Sam!" It was such a proud moment for me—his acting coach!

Then Mr. Owen set up the next scene, one that Sam and I hadn't rehearsed yet. Nathan swaggered across the stage, delivering Danny's lines.

Then there was silence. "That's your cue, Sam," Mr. Owen called out.

Sam cocked his head to one side. "Are you sure you're the coolest guy in school?" he asked Nathan in his nasal whine. "Because you kind of walk like a girl."

I sucked in a breath. That wasn't the next line. What was Sam doing?

"Very funny, Mr. McHugh. But stick to the script please," Mr. Owen directed.

"Sure," Sam answered with a mischievous smile. "I'll stick to the script. Anybody have any tape?"

"What's he doing?" Brittany asked me. "Writing his own show?"

I groaned. "He's messing up everything again! On purpose!"

I was fuming by the time Mr. Owen called for a break. I thought Sam and I had come to an understanding yesterday, but here he was, acting like a clown again.

Sam hopped off the stage and headed out into the hall. *No way,* I thought. *You're not escaping that easily.* "Sam," I called after him. "Can I ask you a question?"

"Ask away," Sam said, smiling down at me.

"Why are you deliberately trying to ruin this show?" I could feel my face flush red.

Sam hooked his thumbs in the pockets of his jeans. "I'm not trying to ruin anything," he said.

His innocent act made me even more upset. "You know, Sam," I said, "you may not care about this play, but there are a lot of people here who do—including me. So why don't you just do us all a favor and read the lines the way you see them on the page?"

Sam didn't say anything. He just looked at me.

"Is that too much to ask?" I continued, my voice getting louder and louder. "I mean, that shouldn't be so hard . . . unless you're a complete *moron*!"

And with that, I stomped away, not giving him a chance to say anything. But I didn't care. I couldn't take it anymore. I wasn't going to let him ruin the show!

"Is there more sandpaper, Mary-Kate?" Jake asked later that afternoon.

"Behind the ladder," I answered as I tacked canvas onto one of the frames we had built. The entire cast was working on the sets. Except Sam. After I lost my temper with him, he stormed out. I was still mad at him. I just couldn't understand how he could be so helpful one minute, and then act like such a jerk the next.

Mr Owen came over to me. "I am really impressed." He stood back and took in the flats. "Nice job, Mary-Kate. You got the supplies here in the nick of time."

"Thanks," I said, glad that things were going smoothly. "But, to be honest, Sam helped out a lot." It pained me to say it. But I knew I couldn't take the credit. "Sam's father is a carpenter, and Sam knew a lot of discount places to call that could deliver fast."

"Well, good for him," Mr. Owen said. "That's what we need—a crew that pulls together."

"If only we had one," I muttered, thinking of the way Sam kept goofing around during rehearsals.

Mr. Owen brushed the dust from his jeans. "Mary-Kate," he said, "let's head into the office. There are a few things we should go over."

"Sure." I handed a bunch of tacks to Jake and followed Mr. Owen into the drama club office. He closed the door behind us. "I don't want anyone to overhear," he explained. "It's about Sam."

"Oh." I groaned.

"Sam came to me today and asked to be dismissed from the play," Mr. Owen said. "When I asked him why, he said that your coaching sessions weren't going well."

I threw up my hands. "We've met twice, I thought we were making progress, but then he—"

"It's not you," Mr. Owen said. "Sam blames himself."

I bit my lower lip, not sure what to say.

"Mary-Kate . . . " Mr. Owen rubbed his chin. "Maybe I should have warned you earlier. I don't know if you understand the nature of Sam's problem."

I frowned. "His problem?"

"Sam has a learning disability," he said. "It's a form of dyslexia. His teachers and counselors have been trying to get Sam involved in some special tutoring, but he refuses to do it."

I gasped. Sam had a reading problem? How awful. How unfair. I had no idea. Then a huge lump formed in my throat and I pressed my hands over my face. I can't believe I called him a moron! Sam had trouble learning, and I made fun of him for it. How could I be so stupid?

"Mary-Kate, I don't want to place the burden on your shoulders," Mr. Owen said. He ran a hand over his bald head. "I just thought you'd be able to help him out a little."

Sure, if he doesn't completely hate me now, I thought.

"The principal asked me to put Sam in the play to get him involved in something," Mr. Owen continued. "I still think it's worth a shot. What do you say?"

"I'll do my best to get him back," I said.

"I knew I could count on you, Mary-Kate."

As Mr. Owen headed back to rehearsal, I leaned back in the desk chair. I had failed Sam in a big way. All of his fooling around with the lines. Switching words around. It wasn't because he was clowning around. It was because of his learning disability.

I screwed up. And, somehow, I needed to make things right again—to apologize—to help Sam get back into the show. I needed to find a way to reach him. . . .

But I wasn't sure where to begin.

chapter eight

"We need a table for six," I told the hostess at All Star Pizza that Friday night. "My name is Ashley."

The hostess smiled at me. "Six?" she said, consulting her list. "Ten minutes, maybe less."

"Perfect. Thanks!" I turned and motioned for everyone to take a seat in the waiting area. Mary-Kate, Brittany, Lauren, and I loved All Star Pizza. Not only did they have killer pies, they also had the coolest sports memorabilia on the walls.

"It'll be a few minutes," I reported to the group, "but we'll have plenty of time to eat and make it to the movie."

"That's good," Lauren said. "I don't want to miss *Attack Force Mars II.* I heard it's even funnier than the first one." She turned to Ben. "Did you see it?"

"We saw it together, didn't we, Ashley?" he asked, smiling at me.

"That's right!" I said, giggling. "And you spurted soda out of your nose! Remember?"

"No way!" Ben laughed. "When?"

"It was during that scene with the aliens in the ice cream parlor." I turned to Lauren. "Wasn't that part hysterical?"

She shrugged. "I don't know," she said. "I've never seen it."

"Oh," I said. "Well, Ben and I had a blast that night." I grabbed a menu and moved past Ben and Lauren. "Let me show this to Mary-Kate," I said. "She always takes so long deciding what to order. Maybe she can get a head start."

I moved through the waiting crowd and squeezed into a seat on a bench between Brittany and Mary-Kate. Jake was leaning against a wall that had a collection of hockey gear bolted to it.

"Hey, Ashley," Jake said. "When are you going to come and help us work on the sets for *Grease*? We've done a lot in the past two days."

"And it's a good thing, since we open on Thursday," Mary-Kate said. She looked worried.

"What's the matter?" I asked.

"Just stressed," she said. "You know, about the show. The costumes. My part. The sets. Coaching Sam . . ."

"But things are going so well," Brittany said. "We're having our first costume fittings at tomorrow's rehearsal, and I can't wait to try mine

53

on. Do you think Christy made me a poodle skirt? Or a skinny, tight pencil skirt?"

Mary-Kate shook her head. "I don't know, but it will be fun to see what Christy comes up with." She pressed her hand to her forehead. "This Thursday! Less than a week until our first show! I don't even want to think about it!"

"The show will be great," Jake said, squeezing her hand.

Mary-Kate shot him a grateful smile. "Hey, I hear tomorrow's pep rally is going to be really exciting."

"You know it," Jake said. "You're coming, right?"

"Are you kidding?" Mary-Kate said. "I wouldn't miss it for the world! Who do you play in the first game?"

"Harrison High," Jake answered. "One of our big rivals."

"Ben's old school?" I asked. I turned to look at Ben and Lauren. He was leaning against a candy-cane-striped pole, nodding as she spoke. They looked adorable together, a totally cute couple.

I had to admit, seeing Lauren and Ben together made me wish I had a boyfriend, too. I hadn't had much luck in the boy department lately.

The hostess called out my name. We followed her to a big booth by a window. Lauren slid into the booth and Ben sat next to her. I slid in next to him.

"Come to think of it, maybe pizza isn't such a good idea," I teased. "Lauren, did you know that Ben is addicted to anchovies?"

"Yuck." Brittany winced as she slid into the booth across from me. "There will be no anchovies on my pizza. Not even on half. I hate those furry, fishy things."

"Really?" Lauren said. "I don't know, Ben. Anchovies? Maybe I can't go out with you after all."

As everyone opened their menus, I laughed. "Ben, remember the anchovy incident?" Brittany and Lauren peered at me over their menus.

"The what?" Brittany asked.

"The anchovy incident. One night when we were out, Ben ordered extra anchovies on his pizza. The owner was so excited. He said he'd never had a customer who loved anchovies as much as Ben did. So he loaded up our pie. When the pizza came to our table, it was more fish than anything else."

Ben nodded. "Yeah. People at tables near ours had to move. They said the fish smell drove them away." He laughed out loud. "That was the funniest night ever!"

Everyone smiled. "I guess you had to be there," I said, chuckling.

When the waitress came, we ordered two medium pizzas with cheese, mushrooms and pepperoni.

"So, Ben, do you have the newest CD from Yellowfellow?" I asked.

"Not yet," he said. "How is it?"

"Awesome," I answered. I turned to the rest of the group. "Ben and I saw them in a concert together."

Jake nodded. "Yeah, I heard they're great."

"They're one of my favorite bands," Ben said. "Do you remember that encore, Ashley? They played past midnight!" Ben sang a couple of bars from one of Yellowfellow's most famous songs. I joined in on the chorus. Then the two of us broke off, laughing. Ben had a terrible voice! I used to tease him about it all the time.

"How about that new single from Cold Day?" I asked him. "They keep playing it on the radio. I can't wait till they release it."

"Cold Day?" Lauren asked. "I've never heard of them."

"They're from Seattle," Ben said.

"Oh, and do you know how they got together?" I asked. I launched into a funny story about the band that Ben and I loved. At one point, I glanced over at Brittany. She was staring at me with a strange expression on her face.

I frowned. What in the world was bothering her?

chapter nine

Jake stretched his arms over his head, then patted his full stomach. "That was one good pizza, huh, Mary-Kate?"

"Mmm-hmmm," I answered. I counted the money for our check one last time.

"Better hurry up, Mary-Kate," Brittany said. "We don't want to miss the movie."

"Take it easy!" I told her. "The theater is right across the street." I finished counting, and looked up in time to see Sam McHugh coming in the door.

He spoke to the hostess, then went to sit at the counter.

I took a deep breath. I had to talk to him. "Okay, that's it with the tip," I said, pushing the money into the folder.

"Great," Jake said. "Let's head out." He stood up and reached for my hand. "Ready, Mary-Kate?"

I stood up. But instead of moving toward the door, I pulled Jake closer to me and whispered, "You go ahead. I'll catch up in a minute."

"Why?" Jake asked. "What's wrong?"

I nodded toward the counter. "It's Sam McHugh. I need to talk with him about his part. Things have been going wrong, and Mr. Owen is concerned, and . . . well, it's a long story."

"Okay . . . ." Jake shot a look at Sam. "I'll wait for you in front of the theater. Don't take too long. The movie starts in fifteen minutes."

"I won't be long," I assured him. "Thanks for understanding."

"I'll be waiting," Jake said.

As he followed the group out, I turned to the counter and took a deep breath. Would Sam be able to forgive me? *Here goes nothing*, I thought as I wove among the tables in the pizzeria.

I approached Sam's seat. "Hey. Mind if I keep you company?" I asked, starting to take the empty stool beside Sam.

"Sure, sit down." Sam waited until I sat down, then said, "But there's ketchup on that seat."

"Yikes!" I jumped up, and looked over my shoulder. It was just my luck, getting a ketchup stain on the back of my new white jeans. *Ugh!*

"Gotcha!" Sam teased.

I breathed a sigh of relief. "No ketchup?" I asked.

"Not even a drop," Sam told me.

"Okay," I said, sitting gingerly on the stool. "I deserved that. I deserved *at least* that."

Sam nodded. "You sure did."

I swallowed hard. "Look, Sam, I am so sorry for what I said at rehearsal today."

"Great. You're sorry and I'm a moron," Sam said. "I guess that evens things out."

"No," I told him. "I was the moron for not understanding your problem."

"Oh, yeah?" He shrugged. "What problem?"

"You know, you cover it up so well," I said. "That whole comic act you pull. I don't think anyone has a clue that you use it to cover up what's really going on. Everyone thinks you're just hysterical."

Sam shifted on his stool. "I don't know what you're talking about."

"Come on, Sam," I said. "I know you have a learning disability. Mr. Owen told me about it."

Sam slid an oregano shaker along the counter from one hand to the other. "So . . . maybe I'm a better actor than anyone realized," he admitted.

"I'll say. I'd give you an Academy Award."

"Really? My parents will be so proud. Finally—an award for something!"

We both laughed, and I felt a surge of relief. "Does this mean you don't hate me?"

"Let's not get carried away," Sam said. "You're still not exactly my favorite person in the world—"

I winced.

"—but you're moving up the list."

I laughed. "So what about the show?" I asked. "Are you going to keep your part?"

When he hesitated, I touched his arm. "I'll coach you—as much help as you need. I'll make sure you memorize all your lines. You're a quick learner, Sam. We'll go scene by scene. Really. Whatever it takes."

Sam's eyes met mine. "You'd do that for me?"

I nodded. "It's the least that I owe you. I mean, if it weren't for you, we still wouldn't have any sets! So . . . please say yes."

"Yeah, okay." He shrugged.

Excellent! I thought. Now that Sam was back in the play, where he belonged, maybe—just maybe—the two of us could become friends!

"Great!" I said, swiveling my stool. "We can pick up our sessions tomorrow, right after the pep rally. Meet me in the auditorium—that way, you can see how the sets are coming along. We've made a lot of progress in two days."

"Really?" Sam asked. "Like what?"

Sam's pizza arrived. As he ate, I gave him a complete update on how the building was going. He seemed impressed. After a while, I glanced down at my watch. Oh, no! I had totally lost track of time. The movie was about to start!

I hopped off my stool. "I'm sorry, Sam, but I have to go. We're seeing *Attack Force Mars II* at the theater across the street."

Sam nodded. "Sure thing. I'll catch you at rehearsal tomorrow."

I zipped out of the pizzeria and tore across the cobbled square to the movie theater. As I jogged toward the box office, I saw Jake waiting by a movie poster, his hands in his pockets.

"Jake!" I called out. "Sorry I'm late!"

"I didn't want to go in without you," he said. His gray eyes were stern. I could tell he wasn't too happy.

"Well, I'm here now. So, let's go," I said, lunging toward the entrance to the theater.

Jake held me back. "It's too late."

"But they always show previews for at least five minutes," I insisted. "Come on."

"Mary-Kate, the show has been running for ten minutes now." He sounded really annoyed. "We missed it."

"What?" Oh, no! I had gotten so wrapped up talking to Sam that I didn't notice I was so late. "Oh, Jake, I'm so sorry. I guess I lost track of the time."

Jake didn't say a word as we crossed the parking lot toward his Jeep. Short of apologizing a *third* time, I wasn't sure what to say to him. "Don't be mad," I said.

He flashed me a look.

"Okay—you have a right to be mad," I admitted. "But let's do something else, something fun. How about the mall?"

"I'm not in the mood."

"Okay, how about ice cream?" I offered. "I'll make you a big hot-fudge sundae at my house."

Jake blinked. "Hot fudge?" He lifted a hand to rub his chin. "Add on some whipped cream, and all is forgiven."

"Mary-Kate, where are you going?" Ashley asked.

It was nearly noon on Saturday and dozens of teachers and students were streaming toward the gym. Today's pep rally would start off the basketball season, and I was totally psyched to root for Jake and his team. But I couldn't resist taking a small peek into the auditorium first.

"I'm going to check on the flats to see if the base coat dried overnight," I called back. "I'll meet you in the gym in two minutes."

"We'll save you a spot," Lauren called as she hurried down the hall. I knew she didn't want to be late. She was meeting Ben, and her face was flushed with excitement.

Just outside the auditorium, I saw the front doors of the school spring open. Sam strolled through them. "Hey," he said casually.

"Hey, yourself," I answered. "Weren't we going to meet *after* the pep rally?"

He shrugged. "I wanted to see the sets. Figured I could work on them while you guys were doing the rah-rah thing."

I smiled. "Come on. I'll show you where they are."

I pulled open the auditorium door, glad that Sam was here. He really *did* care about the show . . . even if he didn't want to admit it.

"Hey, how was the movie last night?" he asked as he followed me into the auditorium. "I heard it's really funny."

"Actually, I didn't get to see it," I said. "I was late. The show had already started, so we didn't go in."

"You were late because of me?" Sam said. "Sorry about that. I'll bet Impenna blew a gasket."

"We were both a little bummed," I said as I bounded up the stage steps. "But we'll get over it." We ducked into the wings. "Most of the sets are over here," I told him. "Let me turn on the lights so you can get the full effect."

I headed toward the fuse box, my sneakers squeaking on the wet floor.

Wait a minute—wet floor?

I gasped, looking down. "What happened here?" I flicked on the lights and saw a shallow river of water stretching across the backstage area.

"Something must be leaking," Sam said, lifting one of the flats. Water dripped from the wood. "This whole area is wet—and the sets are soaked!"

"Oh, no!" I sloshed around, unable to believe my eyes. "The play is five days away and the sets are ruined! What are we going to do now?"

chapter ten

"Hey, Ashley, hand me one of those pom-poms," Lauren said. "I am ready to cheer!"

Ben, Lauren, Brittany, and I were sitting in the bleachers, waiting for the pep rally to start. I leaned over to give Lauren one of the red-and-white pom-poms I brought along for the occasion.

The gym was packed with kids, teachers, and parents. The band played an anthem as people clapped along. Everyone was revved up to kick off the basketball season.

"This is so weird," Ben admitted. "When I was at Harrison High, you guys were our rivals. Now I'm rooting *for* you. I feel like a total traitor."

"Well, you'd better start cheering, Benedict Arnold," Brittany joked. "You're one of us now!"

"Did you catch many basketball games at Harrison last year?" I asked, giving him a pom-pom.

"A few," he said. "Anybody know how the Bayside team looks this season?"

"They finished in fourth place last year," Lauren answered.

"Actually, I think they were third," I said. "That's what Jake told me."

Ben nodded. "What position does Jake play, anyway?"

"Point guard," I said. "Mary-Kate told me Jake is really psyched about this year's team. He thinks they're going to win it all this season."

"Ladies and gentlemen!" The announcer's voice boomed over the sound system. "It's time to introduce this year's Bayside High Jaguars!"

"Okay, guys," I said. "Be sure to cheer really loud when Jake comes out."

Brittany nudged me with her elbow. "Hey, Ashley," she whispered. "Can you tone it down a little?"

"What?" I squinted at her. "It's a pep rally. You want me to be quiet?"

"You're hogging the conversation." She nodded toward Ben. "Give Lauren a break. Back off a little."

I stole a peek at Lauren. She was shaking her pom-pom. She seemed fine.

"Brittany," I said in a low voice, "I'm just being social."

"Maybe too social," Brittany muttered.

I looked at her. "What do you mean, *too social*?"

Down on the gym floor, the announcer introduced another player. Ben and Lauren cheered. But I wasn't paying attention. I was too busy staring at Brittany.

"Think about it, Ashley," Brittany said. "Last night at the pizzeria, all you could talk about were your old dates with Ben. Then, during the movie, the two of you were whispering so much I could barely pay attention to the screen." She paused. "It's like you were flirting with him."

I swallowed hard. What was Brittany talking about? Did she seriously think I was flirting with my best friend's boyfriend?

I was hurt. "Brittany, I can't believe you said that!"

Brittany shrugged. "I call it like I see it," she said.

"Well, you're seeing the wrong thing here," I said. "Ben and I are just friends."

Ben snapped his fingers. "Oh, man, I almost forgot," he said to Lauren, "I've got a surprise for you."

"Really? What is it?" Lauren asked.

"Tickets to Cold Day! They're playing at the Back Door—and we are going," Ben said proudly.

Lauren's face lit up. "We are?"

"Cold Day is amazing," I told Lauren. "Ben and I had a blast at their last concert. You're going to love them."

"It was a last-minute thing," Ben explained. "One of my buddies had the tickets, but he can't use them tonight. So I bought them for us." He slid an arm around Lauren. "This is a great chance to get into their music."

"Tonight?" Lauren's smile faded. "I can't go tonight. It's my little sister's piano recital, and I promised I'd be there."

"No way!" Ben said. His face fell. "Can't you get out of it?"

"I'm sorry," Lauren said. "I just can't. It's been planned for a long time."

Ben winced. "Bummer. And now I've got this extra ticket." He turned to me. "Hey, Ash, you should come. You're into Cold Day."

"I love them," I said. Brittany elbowed me in my ribs, but I ignored her. "I mean, we're friends," I said pointedly. "So if you've got the extra ticket . . . sure. I'll go with you."

"Cool," Ben said. He clapped loudly as another basketball player ran out onto the court. "It's going to be a great show."

I nodded, then glanced over at Lauren. "Hey, Lauren!" I had to shout to be heard. "This is cool with you, right?" I asked.

"Sure." Lauren shrugged. "You might as well go. Why waste a ticket?"

"Great! We'll bring you back a T-shirt," I said. I turned to Brittany. "See? She doesn't mind."

Brittany shook her head. "Don't say I didn't warn you."

"I won't," I answered. I was annoyed. When Brittany got an idea in her head, it was impossible to talk her out of it.

I turned to Lauren. "Are you still coming over this afternoon to do our lit homework?"

Lauren didn't answer. She was staring down at the action on the court. I guessed she couldn't hear me over the noise of the crowd.

Ben nudged me. "Hey! Here comes Jake."

I gazed down at the gym floor. Jake was running across the basketball court, his arms thrust in the air.

"Let's hear it for number twenty-three," the announcer said, "Jake Impenna!"

"Yeah, Jake!" we all shouted, jumping to our feet.

He smiled and waved at the crowd, scanning the bleachers. His gray eyes found our group, and I could tell he was searching for something. His smile faded as his gaze met mine. The question in his eyes was clear. *Where is Mary-Kate?*

I looked behind me, wondering the same thing. Where was she?

❁

"Wow, Mary-Kate. Talk about bad timing." Principal Needham walked through the flooded backstage area. "Ordinarily a leak wouldn't have caused much damage here. But with all your scenery stored in this space . . . " He shook his head. "It's too bad."

Sam lifted a flat from its puddle. "Where did all this water come from, anyway?" he asked.

"The custodian tells me that there's a pipe running through these walls," the principal said. "He'll have his crew here within the hour to take care of the leak. But I'm afraid that won't help you with your scenery. How bad is the damage?"

I shook my head. "It's hard to say."

"Let's put it this way," Sam said. "We'll have to rebuild at least half of the sets."

"And we're totally short on time!" I was in a panic. "The play is five days away. So that means we have to reconstruct, and prime, and paint . . . "

"I spoke with Mr. Owen." The principal pressed his hands together. "He'll be in later for your rehearsal. He can assess the damage then. But he did talk about possibly postponing your opening night."

My heart sank. We had worked so hard on the entire production. It didn't seem fair to have to postpone it now.

"No," Sam said. "No way. We don't need to push the date back."

I turned to him. "We don't?"

"We'll salvage what we can," Sam said, "and I'm really handy. I can get some new sets built ASAP. Really, we've got plenty of time."

I stared at Sam in disbelief. Could we really get it done in time?

"Well," Mr. Needham said, wiping his shoes on the dry floor. "I'm glad to see that this show is so important to you."

"He won't be working alone," I said. "We'll tackle it together—as a team."

Principal Needham smiled. "That's music to my ears. Good luck, kids." He turned and left the auditorium.

I looked around and sighed. "I'm not sure we can actually pull this off," I admitted. "Can we, Sam?"

Sam grabbed a prop table and lifted it out of the watery mess. "Don't worry. We'll be ready by Thursday," he said. "Guaranteed."

❁

"Ashley, are you all set?" Mom asked me later that afternoon. "Do you need anything from the grocery store?"

"No, I'm good to go," I told her. "Lauren will be here any minute."

The popcorn was popped. The lemonade was poured. My books were on the kitchen counter. I had even cracked open a brand new pack of pens. Everything was ready for our study session.

"See you later," Mom called as she slipped out the door.

"Bye, Mom," I said. I snagged a handful of popcorn and popped it in my mouth.

Twenty minutes later, Lauren still hadn't arrived. I wondered what was keeping her. I glanced down at my schoolbooks. The last thing I wanted to do was crack them open and get a head start. But I did have a deadline. I needed to come up with an essay for my English literature class. It was due Monday.

Since I was going to the concert with Ben tonight, it would probably be a good idea to get it out of the way right now.

"Okay, Emily," I said, leafing through our book of poetry, "what would you say your favorite symbols were?"

I was talking to Emily Dickinson, the poet. Unfortunately, Emily couldn't answer. That meant I would have to skim her poetry one more time.

I took a sip of lemonade. Where was Lauren? This would be a lot more fun if she were here. Lauren had mentioned a piano recital tonight, but she hadn't canceled our study date.

So why wasn't she here?

I thought about what Brittany had said. *I'd be upset if you were flirting with my boyfriend. . . .*

No. That couldn't be it, I reassured myself. Brittany was just overreacting. Lauren wasn't upset with me.

Because for one thing, I would never flirt with my best friend's boyfriend. And for another, Brittany was taking everything the wrong way.

Lauren knew I wasn't flirting with Ben.

Didn't she?

chapter eleven

"What's the next line, Mary-Kate?" Sam asked from the bottom of the ladder.

It was Saturday afternoon, an hour before our drama club rehearsal. Sam and I were taking advantage of the time by pulling double duty. While we were repairing the sets, I was helping him learn his lines.

"Your line is 'Ladies and gents of Rydell High, I am most honored to welcome you here today.'"

Sam repeated the line in his squeaky nerd voice.

I laughed. "You've got Eugene pegged! You're definitely going to be a hit."

"I just want to get through the show," Sam admitted as he gently pulled tacks out of a soaked wooden frame.

I dipped my brush into a bucket of green paint. "Your next line comes after the principal makes her announcement over the P.A. system," I said. I stretched to reach the top of the trees I was painting. The ladder I was standing on wobbled as I lost my grip and fell backward.

"Look out!" Sam yelled. He caught me on the way down, breaking my fall.

"Thanks." I smiled. Then I realized that the paint brush I was holding had smacked against Sam's cheek. Green paint dripped down Sam's face. "Uh, Sam? I hope that green's your favorite color, because . . . "

Sam touched a hand to his cheek and stared at his green-tipped fingers. "Aw, man!" he moaned. Then he looked up at me. His eyes crinkled, and a wicked smile formed on his lips.

I laughed, backing away. "Sam, I didn't mean it. Really, I—"

Sam grabbed another brush and flicked it toward me. I stared down at the splotch of yellow paint on my shirt. Then I looked up at Sam. "Okay, that's it!" I yelled. "Sam McHugh, you asked for it!"

"Come and get me," Sam taunted.

I lunged at Sam with my brush. He ducked out of the way—just barely.

"En garde!" Sam called out. Like a sword fighter, he swiped his yellow brush at me.

I jumped back, just in the nick of time.

I caught hold of his wrist and slapped my paint brush down on his arm. "No!" Sam laughed. "No fair!"

"Take that!" I joked.

Just then I heard the shuffle of feet behind me. I turned to see Jake standing in the doorway. "Hey!" I called happily.

Then I noticed Jake's expression. He looked angry.

"What's wrong?" I asked.

"Where were you, Mary-Kate? You missed the whole pep rally."

"I did?" I looked down at my watch. Oh, no! The pep rally had ended an hour ago. "Oh, Jake, I lost—"

"—track of time," Jake finished. "Somehow, I knew you were going to say that."

"I'm sorry!" I said. "But before the rally I came in here to check on the sets, and there was this whole leak and . . . ."

Jake just stared at me.

"I wanted to be there," I continued, "but this was an emergency! Sam and I—"

"Yeah, it sure looks like an emergency," Jake said, glaring at us.

Sam cleared his throat. "So, how did the rally go?" he asked.

Jake ignored Sam and turned to me. "Can I talk to you in private for a second?"

Sam took that as a cue to back off. He went toward one of the wings and started hammering on a piece of scenery.

"Jake, don't be mad," I said. "Believe me, I wasn't happy to see our sets ruined by this flood."

"Right. But you were more than happy to goof off with Sam," Jake said.

"We weren't goofing off," I said, stung. "We were working."

"I heard you both laughing when I came in," Jake said. "And splashing paint all over each other. What else would you call it?"

I glanced over at Sam. Green paint covered his arms and his face. "Is there something wrong with having fun while we work?" I asked defensively.

Jake shook his head. "You know what? Never mind." He cut toward the door.

"Jake, wait . . . " I shouted. But he didn't stop. I stood on the stage, staring, as he disappeared through the auditorium doors.

"Sounds like he's really upset," Sam said as he dragged a piece of the Rydell High gymnasium set toward me.

I swallowed. "He just needs some time to cool down," I said, hoping that was true. "Let's get back to work."

I tried to put Jake out of my mind as I paged through the script. But as Sam and I rehearsed, an uneasy feeling pressed in the pit of my stomach.

"Hello! Anybody home? It's me, Ashley!" I rapped on the front door of Lauren's house.

By then I was totally worried. Lauren hadn't shown up for our study date. It was so unlike her to cancel without calling. I couldn't help thinking that maybe something was wrong. Maybe there was an emergency at home. Or she got into a fender bender or . . .

The front door opened. I breathed a sigh of relief when I saw Lauren standing there, looking completely fine. "What are you doing here, Ashley?"

I gave her a curious look. "Is anything wrong? When you didn't show up for our study date or answer my calls, I thought . . . is everything okay?"

She just looked at me for a moment, unsmiling. Then she said, "Come in."

Immediately, my worry returned. "Okay," I said as I followed her to the living room. "Clue me in. What's going on?"

"I honestly can't believe you don't know," she said. She turned to face me, her arms crossed.

"Know what?" I asked.

Lauren exhaled loudly. "Ashley. You have had lots of boyfriends. Do you really have to flirt with mine?"

"What?" I yelped. "I haven't been— You can't possibly think that I've been flirting with Ben!"

"I don't *think* it," Lauren said. "I *see* it every time you and Ben are in the same room together."

"Lauren, we're just friends," I insisted.

She rolled her eyes. "Right. Friends who talk like there's no one else in the room. Friends who like all the same bands and go to concerts together. How stupid do you think I am?"

"But, Lauren," I said. "I would never do that to you. I was trying to show you I was comfortable seeing you and Ben together. That we could all have fun together because he and I are friends now."

"Oh, Ashley . . . " Lauren shook her head. "That is so phony."

"It is not!" I said. "It's the absolute, total truth!"

Lauren stood up. "You and Ben have such a good time together," she said. "He obviously likes you."

"It's not like that," I said. "There's no spark between us. Remember?"

Lauren shook her head. "Look, Ashley, I can't compete with you. If you really want Ben, just say the word and I'll get out of your way."

"No!" I yelled. "This is all wrong."

"You know what else?" she asked, her eyes shiny with unshed tears. "What really hurts the most is that we talked about this, Ashley. You

said you were happy for me. But instead . . . "
Her voice broke as a tear rolled down her
cheek.

"Lauren . . . "

She turned and ran toward the hall.

"Lauren!" I called, following her to the stairs.

She ran up to her room, slamming her
bedroom door behind her.

"Mary-Kate! Check it out!" I turned to see
Christy Turrel entering the auditorium. She held a
black plastic bag up in front of her. "I have the
sample costumes with me."

The costumes! I had nearly forgotten about
them during my panic over the sets. Thank
goodness Christy was on top of things.

"Terrific! Are those the ones for the Pink
Ladies?"

Christy nodded. "Get ready to be blown
away."

"Why don't Brittany and Danielle try them on
and model them for us?" I suggested.

"Excellent!" Brittany said.

We all gathered around Christy. We couldn't
wait to see what was in the bag.

Danielle frowned. "A garbage bag? Let's hope
it's not a sign of things to come."

Christy totally ignored her as she untied the
bag and took out two bundles. "I've got two

amazing samples here.This one's for Rizzo, and here's Jan's."

"Oh, I love fifties fashion," Brittany said. "Thank goodness I look good in pink."

"I hope you chose the right *shade* of pink," Danielle said, flicking her hair over one shoulder. "I will not go onstage looking jaundiced."

"Don't worry," Christy said. "You're going to love my designs."

Danielle and Brittany made their way toward the ladies' room. Danielle eyed her bundle skeptically as she headed off.

While Brittany and Danielle changed, I talked to Christy about the schedule. "The guys are all set with blue jeans and white T-shirts," I said. "But the show opens on Thursday. Will you need help putting together the other costumes?"

"Nope. It's under control," Christy said.

"We need everything by Wednesday's dress rehearsal," I pointed out.

"I'm on it," Christy said. "That's, like, more than three whole days. It's plenty of time. I'm a fast sewer."

I can't tell you how glad—"

The sound of bells interrupted me.

"Where's that coming from?" one of the other girls asked.

"Someone must have found a bunch of bells in the prop closet," I said.

"Oh, no," Danielle called, stomping onto the stage. "It's worse than that. Much worse."

I gasped when I took in the outfit she was wearing—a cotton blouse with an asymmetrical collar, and a fluorescent, pink satin skirt with a zigzag of fat pink fringe sewn to the front.

As Danielle came closer, I heard that jingling sound again.

I glanced down. "Ummm—Christy? What is that?" I asked, pointing at the row of tiny bells stitched to the hem of Danielle's skirt.

"That is Rizzo's costume," Christy said dramatically. She went over to Danielle and tugged at the cotton blouse. "Looks like a fit to me."

A fit? I thought. *Was Christy serious?* Everything about the costume was wrong!

"Reactions?" Christy asked, beaming.

"You want a reaction? How about—*eeeeeeww!*" Danielle shrieked. "This is nothing like fifties clothes! I mean . . . bells and fringe and—"

"And I look like a freak!" Brittany complained. She stepped onto the stage in a black T-shirt with pink fluorescent circles painted on it. Her pink miniskirt was ringed with black tie-dyed stripes.

"Don't be silly. You look fabulous!" Christy said, her eyes bright beneath her bangs. "Fifties clothes were too defined, but I made adjustments for that. I added my own flair to the costumes."

I pressed my palm to my forehead. I was starting to develop a major headache. The show was only a few days away, and Christy's costumes were all wrong! Somehow I had to convince her to redesign them—fast!

"Christy, these outfits are . . . umm . . . great. Really. But the costumes were supposed to look realistic! We can't use them!"

Christy glared at me. "These costumes are a million times better than the costumes in the movie."

"As a fashion statement, maybe. But the movie costumes were *authentic*," I said.

"Authentic is boring," Christy argued.

"Authentic is what we need," I said.

Christy kicked at the empty garbage bag. "After all my hard work—" She turned and stomped off the stage. "I don't do boring, Mary-Kate."

The auditorium door slammed shut behind her.

"What do we do now?" Brittany asked.

I stared at the outfit she was wearing in total disbelief.

Our costume designer had just quit.

And we had only five days till opening night.

What were we going to wear?

chapter twelve

"Ice cream," I muttered to myself later that night. I poked around in the freezer. "Where did Mom put the ice cream?"

"Hey, Ashley," a voice called. "What are you doing?"

I turned to see Mary-Kate. "Wow! You're late." I glanced at the clock on the wall. "Really late."

"That had to be the longest rehearsal in history," Mary-Kate said. She slumped into a chair by the kitchen table. "And it was definitely one of the worst days of my life!"

Join the club, I thought to myself as I slapped a pint of mocha almond fudge ice cream on the table. I grabbed two spoons from the utensil drawer and handed one to Mary-Kate.

"Straight from the carton?" she asked. "That's pretty drastic. Did you had a bad day, too?"

"Yeah." I nodded. "Hey, what happened to you? Why didn't you come to the pep rally?"

"There was a huge flood backstage," she reported. "All our sets were destroyed."

I sucked in a breath. "Oh, no! What are you going to do?"

"We already started rebuilding," Mary-Kate said. "Sam's being an amazingly huge help. I think the sets will be okay. But I'm not so sure about Jake."

"He's upset that you missed the pep rally?" I guessed.

Mary-Kate nodded.

"I could tell," I told her. "He kept glancing over at us in the bleachers—looking for you."

"I'm going to call him." Mary-Kate sighed. "After some serious sweets." She dug her spoon into the carton. "Hey, what's your deal? Why do you need ice cream therapy?"

It was my turn to sink into a chair. "Ben invited me to a Cold Day concert tonight. But I didn't go."

"Why not?" Mary-Kate asked. "I thought you loved Cold Day."

"I do, but Lauren is really mad at me." I felt my throat tightening. "She thinks I've been flirting with Ben."

"What?" Mary-Kate yelped. "That's crazy."

"That's what I said, too. But then I started thinking about it." I paused for a moment. "I *have* been flirting with him, Mary-Kate. It's been happening all along. I was just the last to realize it."

"Whoa." Mary-Kate gasped. "But I thought you didn't like Ben that way."

"I *don't* like him that way," I told her. "But I think that, deep down, I still wanted Ben to like *me* that way."

"Why?" Mary-Kate asked.

I stabbed my spoon into the rock-hard ice cream. "I've been going out of my way to be bright and chatty and cool around Ben and Lauren. But . . . "

"But what?" Mary-Kate asked.

"I think I crossed the line," I said. "I started taking over conversations—talking about things that only Ben and I had in common. Stuff that Lauren's not into. I just wish I knew why."

Mary-Kate thought for a second. "Maybe it's because of what happened with Brian," she said.

"What do you mean?" I asked.

"Well . . . you thought he wanted to get back together—but it turned out he had another girlfriend."

I nodded, remembering how horrible I felt.

"So maybe, deep inside, you didn't want another ex to like someone else more than he liked you," Mary-Kate guessed.

I thought about it. "Even if that's true," I said after a while, "it's no excuse for hurting Lauren."

"You're right," Mary-Kate agreed. "That's why you have to talk to her. You have to try to explain why you acted the way you did."

I ate a spoonful of the ice cream. "Do you think Lauren will ever forgive me? I don't even know what to say to her."

"Well . . . the truth is a good start," Mary-Kate suggested.

I nodded and for a moment I felt a tiny bit better. At times like this, what would I do without my sister?

"So what else is happening with the play?" I asked, trying to switch the conversation to a lighter topic.

"Well, after I got the set situation under control, Christy Turrel whipped out her costumes."

"Cool! Were they amazing?" I asked.

"Christy went totally wild!" Mary-Kate said. "The costumes had tie-dye and fringe and lots of other stuff. I told her they needed to look authentic, but she said she added her own flair to them. Then she walked out on us."

"You're kidding!" I said.

"I only wish I were!" Mary-Kate buried her face in her hands and groaned.

I mulled over her problem for a second. "I know! Why don't you rent costumes? They've got a lot of fifties stuff at the costume place on Vista Drive."

"That would cost too much," Mary-Kate said. "We're on a limited budget. We're talking sew-it-yourself here, but most of the girls in the cast don't know how to thread a needle."

"So we'll thread it for them!" I said, jumping out of my chair. "Oh, Mom's going to love this! You could have all the girls in the cast come here to sew their costumes. I'll help you organize it. It'll be fun! And Mom is a whiz at the sewing machine. She's always making costumes for those little shows at the day care center."

Mary-Kate brightened up as I laid my entire plan out before her. "What a great idea, Ashley. I can go to the fabric store for material and patterns tomorrow!"

She squeezed my arm. "Thanks. This might just work!"

I smiled. Mary-Kate's problems seemed to be solved. Well, all except for Jake—but I was sure he'd come to his senses eventually.

My problems might not be quite so easy to fix. Either way, I had to see Lauren tomorrow. I only hoped she would forgive me.

The next morning I took a quick shower and pulled on jeans and a ruffled shirt. I bounded down the stairs. I wanted to catch Lauren before she headed out for the day, but I had to eat brunch first. It was a weekly family ritual.

Mom made French toast today—Dad's favorite. While we ate, Mary-Kate told everyone about my idea to sew the *Grease* costumes here.

Mom loved it—just as I thought she would. I got out a pad and pen and started making a list of things Mary-Kate would need to buy and do. Sometimes she needs my help getting organized.

By the time Mary-Kate and I did the dishes, it was almost noon. I hoped Lauren didn't have any plans. I grabbed my car keys and headed out the door.

A few minutes later I turned onto Lauren's street. But the moment I drove up to her house, I felt slightly sick to my stomach. This had to work. If it didn't, I wasn't sure what I'd do.

I parked beside a tall palm tree. Then I went to the side door and rang the bell.

Lauren's mom opened the door. "Hi, Ashley! Lauren's in her room. You can go on up."

Lauren was sitting at her computer with her CD player on. She looked up. "What are you doing here?" she asked, pulling off her earphones.

"I know you're mad," I began. I sank down onto her bed, dropping my car keys beside me. "And now I understand why. I came to apologize, Lauren. You were right." I swallowed. "I *was* flirting with Ben. I want to explain—"

"You can't change what happened," Lauren said. "There's no use getting hung up on it."

"But I kind of need to tell you why I did it," I admitted. "Just so you know I didn't mean to—"

Lauren cut me off again. "You know, I'd rather not talk about it. It's all over, anyway."

"What is?" I asked.

She looked at me. "Me and Ben," she said. "Since you two are obviously so perfect for each other, I decided to break up with him."

chapter thirteen

No, I thought. *This can't be happening!* Ben was Lauren's first real boyfriend, and now, because of me, she had dumped him!

"You can't do that, Lauren," I insisted. "It's a mistake! He doesn't like me. He wants to be with you."

"You could have fooled me," Lauren snapped. "I mean, what kind of boyfriend takes another girl to a concert? And spends the whole night laughing about old times with her? I felt like the outsider whenever you guys were together."

"Ben and I didn't go to the concert," I said. "He went with Todd."

"Really?" She looked hopeful for a moment. Then she shrugged. "The concert was only a tiny part of it. I can't sit around waiting for Ben to get over you."

"No! He likes you, not me," I insisted. "It's just that I kept getting in the way! Can't we talk about this?"

Lauren sighed. "We can talk," she said, "but I've made up my mind. It's over."

No matter what I said, I couldn't convince Lauren to give Ben another chance.

What can I do? What can I do?

The thought raced through my head as I drove my car down the winding streets of Malibu. At first, I wasn't even sure where I was going, but when I turned onto a wide avenue and found myself cruising by Ben's new house, it all made sense.

I had to talk to him and figure this out. I had to find a way to get Ben and Lauren back together.

As I walked up the driveway, I spotted Ben in the backyard. He was dressed in sweats, furiously dribbling a basketball against the pavement.

"Ben," I called. "If you bounce that thing any harder, you're going to crack the driveway."

He hopped to catch the ball, then turned to me. "Hey, Ashley. I'm not in the mood to talk right now. Lauren and I broke up."

"Yeah, she told me," I said. "I was just at her house."

"I can't believe she broke up with me!" Ben wiped a sleeve over his forehead. "It was totally out of nowhere."

"Ben, it was my fault," I confessed. "Lauren thought I was competing with her. She thought that I was flirting with you."

"She did?" He squinted. "But that's dumb. I told her we were over a long time ago."

"She isn't sure you really like her," I said.

"That's nuts," Ben said. He slammed the ball into the pavement again.

"I feel horrible about everything," I said. "And I'm sorry—really sorry. But the thing is, if you care about Lauren, you can't give up on her just yet."

Ben didn't say anything, just kept on dribbling.

I went over and snatched the ball away. "Ben, listen. I have a plan for how you can get her back."

Ben finally looked up at me. "Okay," he said. "Let's hear it . . ."

By Monday afternoon I had talked to every girl in the play about the big "Sew-In" at our house that night. I had already bought patterns, yards of fabric, spools of thread, and even a few cool poodle decorations. With Ashley's help and Mom's expert fingers, everything was ready to go. Now if only I could find Jake and get him to talk to me, everything would be back on track.

Ever since our fight Saturday, he ignored my e-mails. He didn't call me back or answer any of my pages. And every time I stopped at his locker or outside one of his classes, Jake was nowhere to be seen. He was dodging me, I knew it.

When the bell rang for my free period, I shot out the double doors of the school and ran over to the baseball field, where I knew he liked to hang out. But when I got to the field, there was no one there.

I sat cross-legged on the ground and tore at a patch of clover. It was so frustrating that Jake was mad at me for missing a pep rally. I had to make him understand that I wasn't messing around with Sam. But how could I do that if he wouldn't talk to me?

"Hey, Mary-Kate," someone called.

I turned to see Sam crossing the field. He tossed his backpack on the grass and sat down beside me.

"You've got a lot of nerve," he said. "Hanging out here while there's still scenery to build."

"Don't say that." I groaned. "If I have to paint one more panel of Rydell High scenery, my fingers are going to fall off."

Sam laughed. "I'm just teasing. It's under control. At least, the scenery is. But you look like a wreck."

"I'm so stressed," I confessed. "Between the scenery and the costumes . . ." I raked back my hair with both hands. "I may not make it to opening night. I mean, what's next? Will Nathan get amnesia? Will Danielle lose her voice?"

"That might not be so bad!" he cracked.

"Danielle is a great Rizzo," I said.

"Yeah, and she knows it, too!" Sam joked. Then he turned to face me. All of a sudden, he looked serious. "Mary-Kate, I wanted to say thanks."

"For what?" I asked. "You're the one who saved the sets. Without you, there wouldn't be a show this Thursday."

Sam smiled. "It's just that I never thought I could be in a show like this—because of my problem." He paused. "I'm having a great time. And it's because of you. I owe you, Mary-Kate. Big time."

For a second, my heart felt a little lighter. "Thanks for saying that, Sam. This show wouldn't be the same without you."

Sam glanced at me out of the corner of his eye. "Although, you aren't exactly the most relaxing person to be around, you know."

I raised my eyebrows. "I'm not?"

"No. And you can be a little uptight sometimes." Sam gave me a little shove.

"Ouch!" I rubbed my arm.

"You know, I think you need to loosen up a little," he said, shaking me by the shoulders.

"Hey! Stop that," I cried.

Sam laughed. "Make me!"

I tackled Sam and held him down. "I'm not letting you up until you say you're sorry."

"Oh, yeah?" Sam grabbed me under my arms and poked me in the ribs.

I leaped away from him, shrieking with laughter. I am totally ticklish in that spot.

"Mary-Kate?" A familiar voice made me freeze in place.

Oh, no. My head whipped around to face my boyfriend.

Jake shook his head and turned away.

"Wait!" I stood up and ran after him. "We have to talk!" I caught up to him, but he kept on walking.

"Jake!" I said, out of breath. "I've been trying to find you all day. I want to talk about Saturday."

"There's nothing to talk about," Jake said, his mouth set in a grim line.

"No, Jake. Listen to me." I put a hand on his shoulder and he stopped.

"What do you want me to listen to, Mary-Kate? A reason why you always have time to hang with McHugh and not me?" he asked. "An explanation of how the two of you have gotten *close* these past few weeks?"

Close? Something about the way Jake said that word made me stop short. "What are you talking about?" I asked slowly.

Jake crossed his arms in front of him. "Don't worry. You don't have to break it to me. I can figure it out for myself."

"Figure out *what*?" I demanded.

"That you're seeing him behind my back," Jake shouted.

I stood there—completely stunned.

"Jake," I said, "you can't possibly think that—"

"You left me at the movies because you were talking to him," Jake interrupted. "Saturday, you ditched my pep rally for him. I caught the two of you having a paint fight in the auditorium. Then, today, I see you all over each other! What else am I supposed to think?"

I couldn't believe it. After all this time, after all we had been through, how could Jake doubt me so easily?

"Jake—do you really believe that I'm cheating on you?" I asked again. "That Sam and I—"

"I can't believe I didn't see it sooner!" Anger sparked in Jake's eyes. "And what I really can't believe is that you did this after I joined the stupid drama club—just so I could spend more time with you!"

"'Stupid drama club?'" My mind reeled. How could he say that? My face flushed hot as anger flooded through me. I tried to calm myself, but I just couldn't stop the words from coming out of my mouth.

"I am telling you once and for all that I am not seeing Sam behind your back," I said. "And if you can't believe me, then maybe we shouldn't be going out with each other."

"What?" Jake was stunned.

"I mean it," I continued. "If you decide that you can't trust me, then it's over." Tears stung my eyes, but I looked away, not wanting Jake to see.

"Fine," he said.

Then he turned his back to me and walked away.

chapter fourteen

"Look out, Mary-Kate!" Brittany called.

I moved aside as she danced across the stage. The other Pink Ladies danced behind her.

"We go together like changa-langa-langa . . ." Brittany sang, skipping across the stage. She spun on her toes and her pink poodle skirt twirled around her.

It was Tuesday and we were having our dress rehearsal one day ahead of schedule. The costumes had turned out so well that we wanted to try them out right away.

Danielle came up to me, smoothing her "Danielle-pink" pencil skirt as she walked. "I can't believe I'm saying this, but last night was a blast. I never thought I'd actually enjoy sewing. It was nice of your parents to let us use your house."

"They were really great about it," I agreed.

Just as Ashley had predicted, the girls in the cast had lots of fun helping one another cut and baste and sew each other's costumes. My fingertips were still a little sore from getting stuck with the needle, but it was all worth it when the costumes were finished. Dad had even pitched in, ordering pizzas for the whole crew.

"Lucky for us, Mom loves to sew," I said.

"And she's good at it," Danielle said.

"We love our costumes!" Brittany sang as she danced off the stage and joined us. "Everyone is getting into the *Grease* spirit."

"The Rydell High spirit," I corrected her.

"Whatever." Brittany grabbed my hand. "Come on, Sandy, let's dance!"

"Maybe later," I said, pulling back. I was glad the costumes had worked out, but I didn't feel like dancing.

Brittany pulled me off to the side. "Oh, Sandy, you're looking blue." She paused. "It's Jake, isn't it?"

I swallowed, trying to ignore the tears stinging my eyes. "Yes," I admitted. "It's Jake."

After I told Jake that we shouldn't go out with each other if he couldn't trust me, I waited for him to call me, or e-mail me, to tell me that he had come to his senses. That he knew he could trust me.

But he didn't do any of those things. He was even avoiding me at rehearsals.

Did this mean that the two of us had broken up?

❋

"Mary-Kate, meet the newest member of the Bayside High stage crew!" I clapped a hand on Ben's shoulder and nudged him toward my sister.

Ben stepped forward. "Thanks for helping me out, guys," he said. "I just hope this works."

It was Wednesday afternoon, one day until the play's big opening night. I knew I had to get Ben and Lauren back together, and the play would give me the best opportunity to do that.

"Don't worry," Mary-Kate said. "When Ashley comes up with a plan, it's usually a good one." Her long blond ponytail bobbed behind her.

I giggled, taking in her costume. She looked totally great. But it was funny to see her dressed up like a girl from the fifties—complete with poodle skirt and saddle shoes.

"So what is the plan exactly?" Ben asked.

"Well, this is the full dress and technical rehearsal," Mary-Kate explained. "Lauren is on stage crew, and I'm putting her in charge of lifting the full moon during one of my scenes."

"And guess who Mary-Kate's putting in charge of helping Lauren?" I said.

"Me," Ben said. "But how is that going to help?"

"You'll be in really tight quarters," I told him. "So there's no way she'll be able to ignore you. You can tell her how much you want to get back together. She'll have to listen!"

"During the scene, I'll be singing one of the most romantic songs in the play," Mary-Kate chimed in. "It will totally set the mood. Lauren won't be able to resist!"

Ben frowned skeptically. "I hope you're right," he said.

"This is guaranteed to work," I told him. "Trust me."

A little while later, I shook my hands nervously as everyone got in place for Mary-Kate's scene. Mary-Kate had positioned me backstage by the light board. It was the perfect spot to spy on Ben and Lauren.

"You look more jittery than I feel," Mary-Kate whispered. She stood next to me, waiting for her cue.

"I can't help it," I told her. "I screwed up Ben and Lauren's relationship. If I don't fix it, I'll never forgive myself."

"I'm on!" Mary-Kate told me. "Here goes nothing!"

I gave her a thumbs-up as she stepped out onto the stage. I couldn't really see her performance from where I was standing, but I could hear her voice.

As she began to sing, I peeked behind the flats. Lauren and Ben were scrunched in a corner. They were holding a thick rope, which would hoist the large wooden moon over Mary-Kate as she sang.

Oh, no! Lauren still looked angry. She wasn't even looking at Ben.

Come on, Lauren, I silently urged. *Give him a chance!* I held my breath.

Brittany came up and clapped me on the shoulder. "How's it going, Ashley?"

I turned. "Shhh…I think they're about to make up. At least Lauren's looking at him now. Before, she was totally ignoring him."

We watched as Ben talked and talked. Lauren shook her head, then nodded, then shook her head again.

"I wish I knew how to lip-read," Brittany whispered.

Then Lauren laughed at something Ben said, smiling up at him.

"Crew!" I heard Mr. Owen shout from the front of the stage. "It's time for the moon. Where is the moon?"

Ben peeked out from behind the set. "Uh, sorry," he called out. "Which line is our cue again?"

Mr. Owen told him, and Ben gave him the thumbs-up. Then he looked over at me and winked. *YES! My plan worked! Lauren and Ben were back together!*

Now, if only Mary-Kate and Jake could patch things up, everything would be perfect!

chapter fifteen

"How do you feel?" I asked Mary-Kate as she sat backstage, applying her makeup.

It was Thursday night, and Mary-Kate's first performance of *Grease* was about to get under way. Mom and Dad were sitting in the audience, ready to cheer her on. I couldn't wait to see the show she had worked so hard for.

"Nervous. Feel my hands—they're like ice!" Mary-Kate said. "This is it, Ash. No more screwups. Either we're a hit tonight, or we're a total flop."

I squeezed her shoulders. "You're going to be great!"

Mary-Kate smiled up at me. "I hope you're right."

"I know I am," I told her. "Now get out there and break a leg! You are going to be the best Sandy ever."

"Thanks," she said. "You're coming to the cast party after the show, right? Everyone wants to see you. You were so much help pulling the costumes together."

"I wouldn't miss it," I said, heading out of the dressing room. "See you later!"

I turned a corner—and found Lauren standing in front of me. We hadn't spoken in days. Now, standing face to face with her, I felt a little awkward.

"Hey," I said hesitantly. "I was just on my way to my seat."

"Ashley, wait. I have to tell you—I'm sorry. Really. I feel awful about the way I acted. I didn't listen to you, and I took your friendship with Ben the wrong way."

I felt my throat tighten. "I'm the one who should be sorry. After what happened with Brian, I think . . . I think . . . I really wanted Ben to like me—even if I didn't like him back. It was totally selfish."

Lauren gave me a hug. "I understand."

"I promise to stay out of your way from here on in," I told her, squeezing her tight.

"But you're my best friend. I want you to be around!" She gave my shoulders a shake. "Ben spilled the beans. He told me about your little plot to get the two of us back together. Not that I didn't guess it was you already!"

·I laughed. "I guess it worked."

"How could it not?" Lauren asked. "For the two of us to hoist that moon, I almost had to sit on his lap!"

"Attention, everyone! Can I have your attention?" Mr. Owen entered the backstage area. "Places, please! It's two minutes to curtain!"

"I'd better go," I said. I hugged Lauren one last time before I raced out to catch the show.

As I settled in next to my parents, I smiled, knowing that I had done the right thing. Lauren and Ben were back together, and I was free to follow my heart when the right guy came along.

"Excuse me. Is anybody sitting here?"

I turned to find Aaron Moore standing in the aisle. He pointed at the seat next to mine.

"Nope," I told him. "Have a seat."

"Thanks," he said.

I smiled at him, then sat down to enjoy the show.

❀

My heart thudded as we sang the last refrain from the final song of *Grease*. The show had gone well from beginning to end. All my hard work, all the stress, had finally paid off!

The finale ended, and we lined up for our curtain calls. After the bit players, Sam stepped forward in his nerd costume. His eyes widened when the audience went wild.

I laughed. Sam was a total hit. He was so funny as Eugene, he had totally stolen the show!

Then Nathan grabbed my hand, and we took our bows together. As Danny and Sandy, we got the loudest cheers of all.

The curtain fell for the final time—and a whoop went up from the entire cast. We were a hit!

Nathan squeezed me in a big hug. Brittany threw her arm around me. "This is incredible," she told me. "We actually pulled it off!"

"I know," I said. "I can't believe it!"

"Hey, MK!" I turned to face Sam. He picked me up and whirled me around.

"We did it!" Sam exclaimed.

"We did it!" I yelled back.

"This is awesome! I can't wait to do it again tomorrow night." Sam put me down. "I'm going over to thank Mr. Owen. But first, I wanted to say, 'Thanks, Coach!'" He kissed me on the cheek and hurried off.

I glanced up—and found Jake standing in front of me. We froze, staring at each other for what seemed like forever. I gave him a small smile. *This is it*, I thought. This is where Jake kisses me and everything turns out okay.

I waited.

Jake looked at me, his face expressionless. Then he turned away.

Ashley came over and stood next to me. We watched as Jake walked out the stage door. "I guess he's still mad, huh?" she said.

Suddenly, I was tired of it. "You know what, Ashley? I don't care anymore. If he still thinks that I was fooling around with Sam . . . then he doesn't understand me at all. It's over." I blinked back tears.

Ashley hugged me. "I know you feel terrible right now, but for what it's worth, I think you're doing the right thing."

"Thanks, Ashley. Me, too." I took my sister's arm, and we went to join our friends at the cast party.

Find out what happens next in

Sweet 16

Book 7:

PLAYING GAMES

"Ashley, Coffee Heaven is taking over the world!" Mary-Kate groaned. "At this rate there's going to be one on every block!"

"I know." I sighed. Coffee Heaven was fine, but it wasn't *our* place. Not like Click Café.

"At least we can have Brittany's party there," I added. "Tanya said it was no problem. She's not even charging us for use of the room."

"That's cool." Mary-Kate leaned back against the pillows on my bed and frowned.

"Hey, don't get so excited," I teased. "What's the matter?"

"I don't know." She sighed. "Didn't you think Jake looked great this afternoon?"

So that was it. "Sure," I replied. "He usually does."

"Ashley—do you think I made a mistake?" she asked. "Breaking up with Jake, I mean."

I shrugged. "I understand why you did it," I told her. "You started to wonder if maybe he wasn't as nice a guy as you thought."

"Yeah," she said. "But what if I was wrong?"

"I don't know," I said. "But one thing I do know—you two are very compatible."

"How do you know that?" Mary-Kate asked.

"Mostly just the way you guys get along together," I said. "But there's also my Theory of Compatibility."

She sat up. "Your what?"

"Theory of Compatibility," I repeated. "You and Jake score really high."

She raised an eyebrow. "*What* are you talking about?"

I pulled out my math notebook. "I figured this out in math class the other day," I said, flipping open the notebook. "See, there are two categories—Interests & Personality, and Goals & Values." I showed her a graph I'd made in the notebook.

"Most people think it's important to have a lot in common," I explained. "But that's not true— look at Jennifer and Tom."

Jennifer and Tom were seniors at school. They were one of those odd couples who have nothing in common—and I mean *nothing*—but get along great. Jennifer was a vegetarian, heavily into politics and animal rights. Tom was a steak-chomping football player. Nobody could understand why they were together, but they were totally in love.

"So?" Mary-Kate said.

"So I figured out a formula," I told her. "It's not how much you have in common with a guy. It's the *ratio* of common interests to common values. The ratio of Category One to Category Two. Jennifer and Tom have zero interests in common and zero goals or values in common. Their personalities are nothing alike. Zeros across the board. So both categories are even. They're balanced." I paused. "We happened to be doing something with ratios in math class that day."

"You are seriously deranged," Mary-Kate joked.

I laughed. "Give me a chance. Let's say you have five interests in common with a guy, but only one similar goal or value. The ratio would be five to one. That's not good."

Mary-Kate shook her head. "This doesn't make any sense."

I ignored her. "There's one clincher, though. If, completely independently, you and your honey have the same favorite song *and* favorite book, nothing else matters. You're made for each other! You and Jake both love *Great Expectations*, right?" I said, naming her favorite Charles Dickens novel.

She nodded.

"And before you even started going out, you both had the same favorite song!" I finished. "You have the clincher. That means you're a good couple."

Mary-Kate laughed. "You sure are into this theory of yours. You should start a matchmaking service."

"I'll get right on that," I said. "As soon as I find a way to keep Click from closing, and maybe save the world while I'm at it."

"Let's just worry about Click for now," Mary-Kate said. "Though you'd be a great matchmaker, and people love stuff like that."

I could almost see the light bulb flashing over my head.

"That's it!" I cried. "That's the perfect way to bring more customers to Click—and keep it from closing!"

"What is?" Mary-Kate looked confused.

"A matchmaking service!" I said. "I'll start one at Click. Everybody will love it!"

"And you can put your theory to the test," Mary-Kate added. "See if it really works."

"Oh, it works," I assured her. "You'll see."

❀

"We've only got two weeks until Brittany's birthday," I said the next day. "That's not much time."

I glanced at Ashley. If there was one thing we learned from planning our own sweet sixteen, it was that the earlier you start, the better.

Lauren sipped her soda. Ashley and I met her for lunch in the cafeteria to talk about Brittany's surprise party. "Why don't we meet at Click tonight?" she suggested. "We can look it over and decide how we want to set up the party and what kind of decorations we'll need."

Ashley nodded. "Good idea. Should we do a theme party, or—"

I spotted Brittany across the room, bee-lining toward us. "Shhhh . . . Brittany's coming," I interrupted.

Ashley stopped talking. We were all quiet when Brittany sat down next to me.

"Hey there," she said. We grinned at her. I have to admit, it must have looked suspicious. Brittany's no fool.

"Were you just talking about me?" she asked. "You sure are quiet all of a sudden."

"No!" Lauren said, a little too loudly. "We weren't talking about you. Not at all."

"Why would we talk about you?" Ashley asked. "Is there something we should know?"

Brittany threw her a strange look. "Not that I can think of."

"I was talking about Jake," I lied. "And he walked by, and I didn't want him to hear me—"

Brittany glanced around the room. "Where is he? I don't see him."

"He left," Ashley said. "So, what have you got for lunch there, Britt? Vegetable soup?"

"Uh-huh." Brittany blew on her soup and tasted it. She made a sour face. "I give it negative four stars."

"That's what you get for being adventurous," Lauren said.

mary-kateandashley

Sweet 16

(1) *Never Been Kissed*	(0 00 714879 8)
(2) *Wishes and Dreams*	(0 00 714880 1)
(3) *The Perfect Summer*	(0 00 714881 X)

HarperCollins*Entertainment*

PARACHUTE PRESS

DUALSTAR PUBLICATIONS

mary-kateandashley.com
AOL Keyword: mary-kateandashley

mary-kateandashley

mary-kateandashley
TWO of a kind ™

 HarperCollins*Entertainment*

 PARACHUTE PRESS

DUALSTAR PUBLICATIONS

 mary-kateandashley.com
AOL Keyword: mary-kateandashley

TM & © 2002 Dualstar Entertainment Group, LLC.

mary-kateandashley

TWO of a kind ™

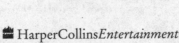
HarperCollins*Entertainment*

PARACHUTE PRESS

DUALSTAR PUBLICATIONS

AOL mary-kateandashley.com
AOL Keyword: mary-kateandashley

Own the Whole Mary-Kate and Ashley Collection!

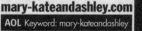

Order Form

To order direct from the publishers, just make a list of the titles you want and fill in the form below:

Name ....

Address ....

....

....

Send to: Dept 6, HarperCollins Publishers Ltd, Westerhill Road, Bishopbriggs, Glasgow G64 2QT.

Please enclose a cheque or postal order to the value of the cover price, plus:

UK & BFPO: Add £1.00 for the first book, and 25p per copy for each additional book ordered.

Overseas and Eire: Add £2.95 service charge. Books will be sent by surface mail but quotes for airmail despatch will be given on request.

A 24-hour telephone ordering service is available to holders of Visa, MasterCard, Amex or Switch cards on 0141- 772 2281.

HarperCollins *Children's Books*